WARMONGERS
AND WANDS

DEBRA DUNBAR

CHAPTER 1

HADUR

*S*moke curled from my bovine nostrils and I stomped the ground in a fit of anger that was far beneath the dignity of my usual behavior—the stomping part, that is. The anger part…well, for a demon of war, I liked to think I was relatively even tempered, but being summoned would annoy even the most stoic of hell's minions.

Actually, my irritation was fifty percent genuine and fifty percent theatrics. It wouldn't do to appear too eager to serve, too hopeful that the witch who brought me here might be interested in a long-term, mutually beneficial partnership, too hopeful that maybe I'd somehow find a witch to bond with. The chances of that happening were pretty much slim to none, though. Summoning had grown increasingly rare the last few centuries. Partnerships, an agreement with a witch that lasted beyond the one-off task, even rarer.

And bonding? It was a fantasy that most demons had realized would never happen.

It wasn't like I'd *never* been summoned before. As a war demon, I'd occasionally been summoned and sent to facilitate the demise of an enemy army, or stir up strife in a neighboring country, although I hadn't been brought out of hell by a witch in over three hundred years.

But this witch…

She had auburn hair and a sweet face. I could see the energy like an aura about her, see it coiling around her arms. Where was her coven? The fact that she'd summoned me alone gave me hope that finally a witch had chosen me to extend an offer of partnership. To bond with a witch would amplify my powers as well as hers. To bond with *this* witch… well, I had some pretty lurid ideas of what else that relationship might entail.

I *was* a demon, after all.

"What is your name?" she called out, her voice husky with an edge to it that made me instantly shed my demon appearance in favor of something more human and hopefully more sexually appealing.

"Hadur." I took a step forward, coming up against the impenetrable ward. "What is yours, witch?"

Her chin lifted and I saw she was young—a woman, but young. "Adelaide Perkins."

"Why have you summoned me, Adelaide Perkins? What task is it that you wish me to complete?"

Normally I would have gone on and on a bit about how I was going to kill her and how dare she bring me from the depths of hell, blah, blah, blah, but this witch was comely and young, so for once I kept my communications unusually polite.

She blinked, those wide brown eyes deceptively innocent. "I did not summon you. Who did so? Who brought you from hell and set you upon my town?"

I frowned, not understanding what she was talking about. "*You* summoned me, witch. I came straight here from hell and am now your captive."

She took a step back, biting her lip. "I did not summon

you. I was gathering herbs for spell and I...I *felt* a presence. But you are restrained in a circle and must answer me truthfully. Thus, I command that you tell me who summoned you and for what purpose?"

I reached out to touch the wards that contained me, wincing at the painful and pleasurable sting of the energy. It felt the same as the spell that had summoned me here, the same as the energy coiling around this witch's arms. Was she lying? If she was, why?

"I have only just arrived, witch. No one has yet given me a purpose or come to me as the one who summoned me from hell. I arrived, and the only being here is you." I tried to smile, tried to appear charming. Since I was a war demon, I'm pretty sure I failed on both those counts. "Release me from your circle. Tell me what task you want me to perform, and release me. I could do so much for you. Together we could be powerful. A witch like you...a witch like you could find more than power in my arms."

The witch stared at me for a moment, a faint blush on her cheeks. Then she turned to leave.

"What is it you want me to do?" I shouted, feeling a bit panicked for the first time in my very long life. This was not the way these things usually went. I was fairly patient as demons go, but I felt very uneasy being trapped in a circle— even if that circle seemed unusually spacious.

The witch hesitated, glancing at me over her shoulder. She muttered something that sounded like, "My mother will kill me."

"I want you to leave." She said the words as if they were a spell. I felt the energy snap around my skin, then dissipate.

"Then return me to hell," I snarled, my interest in her fading. "Banish me. Send me back. At the very least let me out of this damned circle!"

"I...I will be back." She took another step away. "I cannot

let you out, not until I know who summoned you and why. I need to research, to find out some information. Then I will be back."

She left.

And two hundred years later, she still hadn't returned.

CHAPTER 2

BRONWYN

I clinched the last nail and surveyed my work. "Declan, I swear by all that's holy, if you lose one more shoe this week, the next ones I'll put on you will be cement. Then I'm dropping you into the pond."

The centaur chuckled, twisting his torso so he could look down at his hoof. "It's been a wet summer. I'm always standing in water lately. Maybe you should enchant the nails to stay in better."

The problem wasn't the nails; it was his crappy hoof-care routine. Hooves that were constantly in water were soft, and the nails wiggled loose, making the shoe come off and often taking a good chunk of foot along with it. The guy was lucky he had enough hoof wall for me to nail this to.

"Maybe you should apply some Keratex to all four of these suckers every day like I told you to," I scolded.

He sniffed.

"Declan, I mean it. Unless you want to transition to barefoot, that is."

A low vibrating sound came from his throat. In horses, it signaled a sort of wary uneasiness. In centaurs, it was the same as a human disgruntled scoffing noise. I knew why Declan didn't want to go barefoot. All the city streets and sidewalks were tough on unshod hooves. And although he never wanted anyone to know, the centaur was woefully flat-footed, which meant gravel driveways and rocky trails were uncomfortable for him without shoes.

I hid a smile and fitted the metal against his hoof, noting adjustments I'd need to make. Hooves expanded, contracted, and changed shape just like feet did. The difference was *our* shoes went around our feet with adjustments via laces. These were nailed onto his hoof and needed to fit perfectly as well as accommodate any growth in the hoof wall until his next appointment in four to six weeks.

Putting the metal to heat in my forge, I picked up a set of leather pads and threw them into the tub of water to soak. I'd never dreamed my farrier duties would end up being over half my career. As a kid, I'd always loved working with metal —bending and shaping it, enchanting it to hold a spell. Welding, casting, soldering…that's what I'd envisioned when I'd thought about my life's work. But we had a lot of town residents that had hooves. Besides the centaurs, there were a few Pegasus, the unicorns, and even the satyrs. Yes, most of them could manage basic trims on their own, but everyone enjoyed a professional taking care of things—especially when it came to shoes.

Human farriers came into town, but they'd promptly forget about the interesting creatures that were their clients the moment they crossed through the wards out of Accident. It made record keeping and scheduling problematic. And while we did have humans who permanently lived in Accident, none of them were trained in hoof care.

As a teenager, I'd hung out with a few of the farriers when they were working and tried my hand at a few rudimentary shoes, filling in when there was an emergency and a client couldn't manage to bring a farrier into our town. You wouldn't think there would be that many hoof-emergencies, but let me tell you, these centaurs were especially prone to throwing a shoe, getting an abscess, and the occasional laminitis episode that require specialized supportive footwear. Or hoofwear. These centaurs…spring grass really was their Kryptonite when it came to their hooves. I could lecture all I wanted, but each spring I ended up with three or four clients complaining about heat and pain in their hooves. Bar shoes, reversed shoes, you name it. I'd become somewhat of an expert before I'd been able to legally drink a beer.

By my sixteenth birthday, I'd started driving outside Accident to apprentice to a farrier, and at seventeen I was enrolled in formal training. I still attended the occasional seminars and conferences, although I had to be a bit cagy about the types of "horses" I shod and trimmed.

Outside of my farrier duties, I welded pipes, manufactured stock gates, and did custom ironwork. And in my spare time, I made metal art—sculptures and wind chimes.

Spare time. I had a lot of that because my social life was zilch. Less than zilch.

"Saw the shoes you put on Corianna the other day," Declan commented. His voice was carefully casual, which clued me in that he'd been more impressed by Corianna's shoes than he wanted to let on.

I hid a smile and grabbed the tongs to pull Declan's shoe from the fire. "You want pink as well?" The female centaur had hot pink shoes that contrasted with her fancy, painted hooves—creamy white with little pink hearts on the front. I wasn't exactly an artist when it came to painting, but I liked Corianna, and we'd had a sort of girlfriend night last week. She got a mani-pedi with special polish and pink shoes. I drank wine and got to hear all the gossip.

No, I didn't paint my nails. I don't think I'd painted them

since I was thirteen. When you work with metal every day, it seems kind of silly to have long, red nails.

When you go home alone to an empty house every night, it seems kind of silly to have long red nails, too.

"Not pink. And no little hearts. They look pretty on Corianna, but I want something manly. Stallion-like."

Of course. I admirably restrained myself from an epic eye roll. "So, what were you thinking of?"

"Maybe red?" he asked hopefully.

"Corianna's shoes are aluminum, Declan. I need to hot-shoe you, so I can only do steel. But…" I paused for dramatic effect, noting that I had the centaur's rapt attention. "*If* you can get your hoof walls in better shape, I might be able to use those new plastic shoes. They come in different colors. I've been told they're very comfortable, too. Like walking on clouds."

Declan sucked in a breath, his eyes sparkling. "I'd like that."

I hammered the shoe I was working on into shape, holding it up to make sure it was just right. "Keratex, Declan. Every night. And try to stay out of the marshy areas."

He nodded, forelock drifting across one dark eye. "Red shoes, and you'll paint my hooves glossy black?"

I walked over to him, eyeing the centaur. He was gorgeous and he knew it—wavy black hair, golden-brown skin, and a rich deep bay on his horse half. His black tail matched the hair on his head and was long enough to brush the ground. Red shoes would make a statement. They'd be gaudy as all heck on his brown-and-black self, but they'd make a statement. And Declan was all about making a statement.

"You've got a deal. Red shoes and glossy black hooves."

Twenty minutes later, I'd reset all the centaur's shoes and watched him walk and trot around the yard. There was a low rumble of thunder off in the distance, and although there weren't any dark storm clouds in view, the sky had an odd yellowish cast that I wasn't liking.

"These feel great. Thanks, Bronwyn, as always."

I waved his words off, happy to be of help—although I didn't work for free. Declan made good money licensing his digital paintings and he always sent me my payment electronically. Other clients paid me in trade, or sometimes cash. Being a bit isolated here in Accident meant we'd all become creative when it came to the payment methods we accepted. For instance, I pretty much had an open tab at Pistol Pete's so large that I doubted I'd go through it in my lifetime in return for the spell I'd cast on one of his bar rags. He'd been having trouble keeping the peace with all the various folk that liked to come by for a drink and the music and needed something to get their attention and respect. Hence the enchanted towel.

Fear the towel.

I told Declan goodbye after scheduling him for another call in six weeks, then hopped in my truck, eyeing the western sky. Normally I'd just head home, but I had one more call to make, and I'd put this off longer than I should have. With a sigh, I threw the truck into gear and headed down the road, winding my way up Heartbreak Mountain.

Normally, I didn't mind doing work for the werewolf pack, but the last few months they'd turned into two warring packs. Which was quite a bit worse than one warring pack. There were those who supported Clinton, and those who supported Dallas. I didn't support either of them, but out of the two I figured Dallas was the least problematic. The old wolf was a lecherous asshole, but he was old enough to be a lazy lecherous asshole, so he didn't cause quite as much trouble as his son Clinton. Clinton was less lecherous than his father, but more than double the asshole. I'm pretty sure

Dallas in his youth had been just as bad, but he must have mellowed a bit with age, because he tended to stay on the compound, outside of a few days around the full moon, and limit his asshole-ness to those in his pack. Clinton, on the other hand, liked to come into town every day and subject the rest of us to his rude temper and disregard for others' property and rights.

My eldest sister, Cassandra, had finally gotten pissed off enough to take her rightful position as head-witch of Accident and had come down hard on the werewolf clan. But part of the joy of living in a town full of supernatural beings was knowing what to allow as a matter of culture and autonomy and what rules needed to be obeyed for the common good, no matter how much certain folk screamed and cried.

There'd been an incident. Cassie had intervened. She'd had words with Dallas and more words with Clinton. They'd grudgingly accepted her rules and for a few weeks, everyone in Accident and the surrounding area had lived with a sort of icy calm.

Then the calm had ended. Some of the werewolves sided with Clinton and some with Dallas, and the pack was split in two.

Now we had what amounted to a war on the mountain. Nothing had been set on fire, and the violence hadn't spilled into the town proper, but there was definitely violence. Cassie felt we needed to let the werewolves sort this out for themselves, and as long as no one outside of their pack got harmed, then we should let them resolve their issues on their own.

I wasn't sure I agreed with that. Why couldn't we just have two werewolf packs up on Heartbreak Mountain? Or three? Why couldn't people, or werewolves, just get along?

This war among the werewolves was one of the reasons

I'd been avoiding this job. But it was August and getting on toward butchering time. The main pack had a small herd of cattle that grazed on the south side of the mountain and each fall they butchered, selling a good portion of the meat to the town and keeping the rest for the pack to eat through the winter. As much as they liked to hunt, knowing there was a freezer full of roasts and steaks to come home to made the hunt season more of an enjoyable event and less a desperate starvation-fueled one.

Those butchering sheds? They were full of equipment used to slaughter and process the cattle and anything else the werewolves wanted to eat. And evidently a swing-arm on one of the lines had snapped free, and the scaffolding used for hanging the meat had proved not adequate for the weight of the cattle. So here I came to the rescue. Bronwyn, the welder.

I called the compound as soon as I left Declan's to let them know I was on my way. Stanley met me outside the butchering shed. The "shed" was the entire lower half of a barn, squeaky clean with drains in the cement floors and a walk-in refrigerator in the corner. It reminded me of a meticulously maintained torture chamber with all the stainless steel, the iron hooks and racks, the huge blackened cauldrons in the corner. Stanley showed me what needed to be repaired and rebuilt, and I started. The werewolf stood by, watching me as I fired up the torch and got to work on the swing-arm. It was weird having him hovering around like he expected me to steal something. What the heck was the guy's problem? Did he think I was going to run off with a cauldron? Figure out some pack secrets and sell them to the other "team"? Maybe he had a thing for tall, thirty-one-year-old witches with muscles and a few extra inches around their midsections? If so, then he was the first.

My thoughts drifted to my sister Cassandra and her

demon boyfriend. Lucien was smoking hot. I mean, when he looked like a human, he was smoking hot. I'm pretty sure when he looked like a demon, he was terrifying. Either way, I liked him. He was a good guy, which was kind of a weird thing to think about a demon. He was devoted to Cassie, and that was one of the main reasons I liked him. She'd had a tough life, and her last boyfriend had been a 'ho of a panther shifter. Lucien made her happy, and it was good seeing her happy for once.

Good, except I couldn't help a twinge of jealousy when I saw how she looked at the demon, and how he looked at her. They'd do cute little things when they were helping each other with dishes or cooking. There was a back-and-forth banter between them, an intimacy that revealed itself with teasing words and flushed faces and the frequent touch. I so wanted that, but in all my thirty-one years, I'd never had a boyfriend. I'd never even had a guy try to kiss me or ask me on a date. It's like I was invisible to them as anything except an occasional drinking buddy or someone to call when the swing-arm bent in their butchering room.

I glanced over at Stanley and saw him leaning against the wall with his arms folded across his chest, a bored expression on his face as he stared out the window. I'll bet if I stripped off my tank top right now and started welding in my bra, he wouldn't even glance my way. Not that I was interested in Stanley, but it would have been nice to have someone look twice at me for once in my damned life.

But enough of the pity party. I had a job to do here. And after that, I was going to head home to warm up some pork barbeque, pull that bottle of Syrah out of the wine rack, and watch some old movies.

Maybe I should get a cat. Or two. Or a dog. I could take the dog on calls with me to keep me company. Yeah. This weekend, I'd head over to Pitswitch and see what they had at the animal shelter.

The swing-arm didn't take me long to fix, but the hanging rack was a real bitch of a job. An hour in and the rumble of thunder in the distance was becoming more noticeable. Stanley seemed to be close to dozing off while standing, but showed no sign of leaving his post. As I was finishing up, the werewolf suddenly jerked to attention. A few seconds later, I discovered why.

A man walked through the doors—a man with long silver hair and a reddish-blond beard. He was tanned, his face lined and creased, but still attractive in an uber masculine, older-guy kind of way. He was tall with broad shoulders and walked with the sort of attitude that instinctively made people get out of his way.

Dallas Dickskin, the alpha of the werewolf clan.

Yeah, Dickskin. I kid you not, that was really their last name. And no one teased them about it. Well, at least not to their faces.

The senior werewolf ignored the younger one, made an elaborate show of checking my work, then made a more subtle show of checking me out. Dallas was an obsessive womanizer. Werewolves were sticklers when it came to the females having physical relations with anyone besides a male werewolf, but the males weren't held to the same standards. Dallas was legendary for feeling up every woman he met and doing his damnedest to sleep with them. He even hit on Cassie, and my eldest sister was the most powerful witch Accident had seen since Temperance Perkins founded the town. In a fight between the two, Dallas would have ended up a pile of smoking ash, especially since my sister had taken up with her demon lover who acted as a sort of power amplifier for her. That still didn't convince Dallas to keep his hands to himself. Like I said, he hit on every woman he met.

Except me.

"Almost done here?" he grumbled, the cursory once-over he'd given my physical form ending without the slightest spark of interest. The werewolf didn't try to hug me, or touch my ass, or even shake my hand. Not that I was really lamenting not being sexually assaulted by this asshole. It just brought home to me how very undesirable I was.

Which was twisted. I probably needed therapy. I'd get right on that after I adopted a dog and a cat.

"Yep." I checked the weld and started to pack up. "How's the weather look out there? I heard thunder earlier."

"Storm coming. You better hurry if you want to make it off the mountain before it hits."

That got me moving. The roads on the mountain were dirt and rock, and the whole area was prone to flashfloods and washouts. I had absolutely no desire whatsoever to spend the night here in the werewolf compound waiting for the storm to pass and for them to repair the roads enough to get my truck through. Stanley and Dallas made no attempt to help me, watching as I put everything away and gathered my gear up. Their presence still gave me that weird feeling, as if they were making sure I didn't steal anything. It made me wonder what the heck they were keeping in this butchering shed or what I might see that they didn't want me to see.

Stupid paranoid werewolves. As if I gave two shits about their feuds. As long as they steered clear of the rest of the town, and as long as I got paid for my work, they were free to kill each other off.

Paid. Which reminded me...

"Cash, check, or trade?" I asked, knowing that the were-wolves wouldn't be paying like Declan had. First, they weren't the most technologically savvy beings in Accident. Secondly, the cell service on this mountain was total crap. You were lucky to get a faint one bar if you stood on a cliff and held your phone up above your head while on your tip-toes.

"Quarter of beef and a case of apples?" Stanley offered.

I quickly calculated the value in my head. "Throw in some of that salsa you guys traded to Pete and it's a deal."

The younger wolf cast a quick glance toward his alpha. Something beyond my ability to detect passed between them and Stanley nodded. "I'll have someone bring it down the mountain by the end of the month, soon as we get butchering well underway."

"No hurry." They'd need all hands, or paws, for harvest and processing their beef and pork, and I'd need to figure out where the hell I was going to put a quarter of meat. Might be time to buy a second freezer.

A quarter of beef for a single woman. Well, a single woman and possibly a dog or a cat. I'd never be able to eat it all. Good thing I had six sisters to share the bounty with.

The two werewolves followed me out to my truck, watching impassively as I loaded my equipment and closed up the back. The sky was black and eerily still. A fat drop of icy rain hit my arm.

"Well, been nice doing business with you fellas," I lied. It wasn't that I hated werewolves. They were just weird and getting up and down this mountain of theirs was a pain. "Stanley. Dallas. Later, gators."

They nodded and grunted in reply and I climbed in the cab of my truck, pulling out of the compound just as the skies opened up.

I hesitated for the briefest of seconds, considering whether I should turn around and ride the storm out in the compound. I really didn't want to stay there. The truck was in good shape and fully capable of navigating muddy roads. If I took it slow and easy, I'd make it down to the main roads just fine. And if things got too hairy, I'd pull over and just sit it out.

So, I continued, inching my way along the narrow switchbacks, barely able to see the road ahead from the torrential rain. The lightning and thunder had started up again, merged together into a continuous light show and constant crack and rumble of sound. Worried about the sharp curves ahead and my ability to see in this crazy storm, I eased my foot onto the brake pedal.

It went to the floor. The truck kept going. I yanked on the emergency brake, but nothing happened. The truck began to pick up speed, and I frantically ground it into a lower gear, looking for a place to run my vehicle into a bank or even a tree. Crashing my truck was a better option than heading into the steep part of the mountain with no brakes and limited ability to see.

The rumbling grew louder, and I suddenly realized the noise wasn't from the thunder. My breath caught in my throat as rocks began to hit the truck. I felt the vehicle slide to the left, pushed by the rockslide I couldn't even see through the pouring rain. In vain, I pumped the brakes and jerked the wheel. The truck tipped and for a fraction of a second, time seemed to be suspended. I thought of my childhood, of reading books under the covers with flashlights in the bedroom I shared with my eldest sister. Getting up early and making pancakes for everyone before we all left for school. Helping Cassie with the wards. Crying out by the boathouse when Mom left, hoping no one would find me and see.

Shit.

I was going to die.

And my greatest concern was that my sisters would be devastated. Especially Cassie. We'd always been so close. I'd never get to hold my nieces and nephews, never get to give the toast at Cassie's wedding.

I was going to die.

The truck rolled and smashed downward. Glass shattered. I felt as if I were in a rock tumbler, or a rollercoaster gone crazy, flailing about, the seatbelt cutting into my chest. Metal screamed and groaned, and the blackness overtook me while the truck continued to fall.

CHAPTER 3

HADUR

*T*he raccoon came through the dog door, dragging a plastic shopping bag behind him.

"What do you have for me today, Diebin?" I stooped down to pick up the bag. This was my routine. Diebin would go into what I assumed was a nearby town once or twice a day and bring back items for me. Food. Tools. Clothing. Useless brightly colored plastic things.

It was the books, magazines, and newspapers I appreciated the most. They kept me occupied. They let me know what was happening in the world outside my summoning circle. They kept me from going crazy.

Well, except for those Tiger Beat magazines. They actually made me crazy.

"What is Shawn Mendes up to now?" I asked the raccoon as I pulled one of the magazines from the bag. I'd hoped for a GQ, or a Men's Health. This month was supposed to have a list of top abs and arms exercises and I didn't want to miss it.

But Tiger Beat it was. Along with the magazine was a can of something called Chicken a la King, a game controller for an Xbox, a pump for inflating basketballs, a set of pillow cases, goldfish food, and a giant-sized Snickers bar.

"Nice haul," I told him.

The raccoon stood on his hind legs and waved a paw at me.

"Okay, okay. Keep your fur on." I opened the Snickers bar, breaking it in half and giving one portion to my furry friend. Then I sat down at the table with my half of the candy and the magazine. Diebin had brought back three pounds of stew meat and an assortment of vegetables on his run last night, and those were now cooking in a pot over the fire. Between the two of us, we'd managed pretty well over the last two centuries. I'd built this cabin and the tables and chairs; he'd furnished it with stolen stuff from the locals and lately from some place called Walmart which seemed to carry everything a demon could want and a whole lot of stuff I didn't want. Like this game controller. I didn't have an Xbox, and even if I did, I didn't have any electricity to run it. Which was a shame because those electronic games looked like they'd be fun— more fun than this last issue of Tiger Beat, anyway.

The magazine and the candy bar didn't last long. I neatened up the cabin a bit, then headed outside for a loop around the narrow confines of what had become my cage. There was some thunder off in the distance, the sky taking on a faint yellowish tinge that heralded a coming storm. I roamed the very familiar woods around my cabin, looking up the cliff face toward the mountaintop, then wandering to the other side and a partial view of the valley below. The summoning area was in a plateau on a heavily wooded mountain. At first, my days here had been deathly quiet aside from the animals, but in the last century I'd been able to hear the sounds of mechanized equipment both up on the mountain and down in the valley. At night, I could see the faint lights of a town far below me and off into the distance. They'd always been there—a few golden pinpoints in the beginning that had become a splash of light in the last century. I'd watched the town broaden, populate, grow—its story only told to me by faint noise carried on the breeze and the increasing nighttime lights.

When would that witch return? When would anyone come? Each year it became more and more difficult to keep myself from sinking into despair, from destroying everything in my summoning circle in a fit of rage. Was I to remain here forever? Alone, trapped, with nothing to entertain me besides a raccoon and an occasional magazine?

I sat and watched the storm roll in from the distance, trying to keep my hopes up that eventually someone would return to free me. As the first fat drops began to fall, I headed back to my cabin to give the stew a stir and find something to occupy myself. Diebin had brought some batteries last week that fit the cassette player, so I put those in and looked through my collection of tapes. They were all old and starting to fray. It seemed they were out of production as Diebin had not brought me any replacements in the last few decades.

But for now, I had Doobie Brothers, a candle that smelled like sugar cookies, and a dinner I was looking forward to. I headed over to my cache of books, trying to decide what to read as the storm hit and shook the cabin.

Thunder crashed, one after another, then I heard a noise that sounded similar to the thunder.

"Rock slide," I told Diebin, pulling a book from the shelf. They happened on occasion, sometimes large enough to launch boulders through the boundary of my summoning circle. Unfortunately, the rocks and mud and fallen trees did nothing to break the magical borders. Nothing did, although in the past few years I'd sensed a weakening of the perimeter. If no witch came to free me, perhaps in three or four hundred years, the barrier would be weak enough for me to escape.

It was things like that which gave me hope, which helped me hold on.

I felt the crash of rocks through the magical barrier and grimaced, realizing that this was a huge rockslide. The noise sounded oddly metallic, echoing across the plateau and followed by the thump of trees cracking and smashing into each other from the impact.

Then I felt something that nearly brought me to my knees —magic. Not just any magic, but witch magic. She was here. In the middle of a storm, with the rockslide, she'd arrived. My witch was here to save me.

I threw the book aside and ran from the cabin. The cold rain pelted me, wind knocking me back a step. I doubled over and pushed on, determined to face my witch at the edge of my circle, to plead for release. I'd do anything for her—be anything. I'd partner with her, I'd bond with her, I'd grant her immortality, grant her every wish. I'd do anything if only she set me free.

I'd expected to reach the edge of my boundary and see a witch standing there in a glow of light, wind and rain blowing her hair and clothing as she channeled it all in a stream of power. Instead I found rocks and broken trees and a metal box similar to what I'd seen in the magazines.

Correction—two metal boxes. The first one was a twisted broken heap that I believe would have been called a truck. The other was attached behind it, a square metal container that looked to be some sort of trailer. The trailer had broken open and there were metal objects strewn about—a good many of them outside the limits of my circle. I squinted at the truck and trailer, waiting for the witch to appear. I could feel her presence, sense the intoxicating power of her energy.

She was here, inside the truck, no doubt waiting to make an entrance.

When the witch didn't appear, I cautiously approached. It would be disastrous to anger her, but she was inside my circle and after waiting over two hundred years, I was impatient.

"I am here, my witch," I called out over the storm. She didn't answer, so I grabbed hold of the door and pulled. It didn't budge.

What was her truck doing down here, smashed and covered in rocks and trees? She was a witch. Surely, she wouldn't have been caught in the rockslide? Unless the rockslide had been caused by a rival witch. Suddenly the storm took on whole new meaning. I put my demon strength to use and yanked on the door. The handle broke off, so I gripped the sides and pulled it off its hinges.

The woman inside groaned, turning her head to look at me. It was then I realized that she was hurt, in pain, wedged in this broken truck and held as tightly as if it had been a prison.

Her eyes met mine, and I felt a jolt that shook me to my core. A witch. My witch. She was older than when she'd been here before. Her reddish-brown hair fell just past her chin, her skin a golden tan. She was beautiful. So very beautiful. Even injured, she took my breath away.

I knelt beside her. "You came back. You came back for me."

A tiny frown creased her forehead. "I need…I need help. I'm hurt. My legs are stuck. Can you call someone?"

Call someone? I could shout with all my might, and no one would hear me, especially over this storm. Did she mean those communication devices I'd seen advertised in the magazines? Diebin had brought a few of them to the cabin and I'd never managed to get them to work.

There was no need to call anyone. She had me, and I do would everything for her. I would free her, take care of her, give her everything in my power to give. I would serve her, be her devoted partner and bond-mate. I'd be hers for all eternity in the hope that she'd find me worthy, that she would free me.

My witch was here. My witch had finally returned. I nearly wept at the thought.

CHAPTER 4

BRONWYN

I opened my eyes, feeling the wind and rain lashing at my face. Blinking a few times, my eyes adjusted and I realized even through the storm, I could see my shattered windshield, the tree branches and leaves protruding through into the cab of my truck. The airbag sat like a deflated balloon against my bent steering wheel, splotched with something that I was pretty sure was blood. My seatbelt was on, and when I tentatively went to unhook it, I found the buckle was stuck.

Everything hurt—hurt so much that trying to unhook my seatbelt had sent a stab of pain through my chest so sharp that I'd nearly passed out.

I was wet, and I wasn't sure how much of that was rain and how much was blood. Each breath was agony. The front of the truck had smashed in, the dash pressing against my lower half. I was afraid to move my legs—afraid that the sharp ache in my calf would escalate into something worse. Were there splintered bones poking through flesh? Limbs in the back seat? Guts spilled out through a hole in my abdomen? Every horror movie I'd ever seen was playing through my mind right now and all I could do was take slow careful breaths and try not to panic.

This tough welder girl was scared. A fact which would surprise anyone except my sisters who knew that under the brawn and cheeky swagger was a total wimp who could be brought to her knees by a papercut or a wasp sting. This? I didn't want to know. I just wanted to close my eyes and wake up when it was all over and I was in one piece again.

But that wasn't going to happen. My truck was most likely down in some ravine. The werewolves wouldn't think to come look for me. My family wouldn't notice my absence for a few days. I'd need to gather some courage and assess my physical condition, then decide how the heck I was going to get out of here and somewhere I could call for help.

I tried again to unhook my seatbelt, whimpering in pain as I shifted to the side. It was truly jammed. And worse, it had become clear to me that my legs were not only trapped under the twisted dash, but one was definitely broken. Sitting back, I realized that even if I could get the seatbelt free, I'd have to deal with the hunk of metal trapping my legs. Then if some fricken miracle occurred and I freed my legs, I'd be facing an agonizing one-legged hop out of the woods and up the side of the mountain.

Yeah. No.

I looked for my purse which was nowhere to be found. Who knows where it had ended up as my truck had rolled down the hill. The contents were probably spilled all over the cab, and maybe even across the mountainside. Yep, I was pretty sure that was a lipstick down on the passenger-side floor.

Lipstick. Don't judge me. I sometimes wear lipstick, although in reality it's more like tinted Chapstick. When you work outside all day, lips get chapped.

Okay. Focus. I couldn't sit here cold and wet in my

smashed truck with injuries for days, praying that someone would manage to notice I was missing and track me down. I felt around, hoping that maybe some of my purse contents had landed near me and nearly cried from relief when I realized the multitool in my driver's door pocket had somehow not been flung around the cab when I'd crashed. With shaking hands, I pulled it out and began sawing at the seatbelt.

Those suckers were tougher than I'd ever imagined, but using the little saw on the multitool, I managed to disengage myself from the belt. Bruises. Cuts. I was pretty sure I had a cracked or bruised rib or three. My leg… I tried to pull free from the twisted dash and nearly vomited in pain.

Guess I was back to waiting a couple of days for someone to rescue me. Maybe once daylight hit I'd be able to figure a way to get my legs free. Unscrew the dash with the multitool or something like that. Yeah. That was totally plausible. And in the meantime, I'd just freeze to death in the chill of the night, wet and injured in a broken truck.

I blinked back my tears, gripped the multitool tight and closed my eyes, hoping when I opened them, all this would have been a bad dream.

Instead I opened them to the sound of something against the door. Before I had a chance to ready my multitool for defense, the truck rocked from side to side. I gasped in pain, everything going momentarily black. When I could see again, I heard the squeal of twisting metal and turned to see the driver's side door to my truck being torn off the hinges.

I'll admit to being momentarily annoyed that someone was tearing the door off my truck, but I quickly remembered that was the least of my worries. The truck was most likely totaled as well as my little trailer with my forge and all my tools. I was injured and trapped. Someone ripping the door off my truck meant I wasn't down in this ravine alone. Had the paramedics found me? I blinked and tried to focus, expecting my sister Ophelia's face to appear in the spot where my driver's side door had once been.

A face did appear but it wasn't Ophelia's, or anyone else I knew from Accident. This was a man with a tangle of dark wavy hair, a tanned face with a thick black beard, and light brown eyes under dark brows. There was a strange light filtering through the trees behind him that haloed his head, bringing an otherworldly feel to what had become a really shitty day.

Who the hell was this guy? I knew everyone in Accident and I'd never seen this man before. Was I dead? If so, I'd expected to meet a geriatric Saint Peter at some pearly gates in the clouds, not be yanked from the wreckage of my truck by this Jason Momoa look-alike.

Mmmm. Jason Momoa. Now *that* would be heaven.

The man stared down at me, astonished, as if he'd never seen a woman in a wrecked car before. Guess that meant he wasn't a paramedic. Or Saint Peter. He reached a hand toward me, swiping a finger along my cheek. It was red when he pulled it away. Rubbing the bloodied finger against his thumb, he frowned.

This whole thing had taken a surreal turn—as if things could get any more surreal than the brakes going out in my truck during a thunderstorm, getting caught in a rockslide, and being hurtled down a mountain.

He looked up from his fingers, his eyes meeting mine. "You came back."

His voice was deep and raspy, just as mesmerizing as his appearance.

"You came back for me," he repeated. Then, before I could reply that I had no idea who he was, the man reached in and pulled me from the truck.

Actually, it wasn't that easy. He went to wrap an arm

27

around my waist and I screamed. The seatbelt was a dangling, sawed-in-half strap. The air bag was a chalky deflated mess on the steering wheel. Something in my chest had stabbed me like a knife when he'd touched me, and my legs were still pinned under the mangled dashboard.

With a mumbled apology, the man grasped the steering wheel and yanked it from the car. Then he took the bottom part of the dash with both hands and twisted it upward. I inhaled sharply, feeling the pressure leave my legs, only to be replaced by agonizing pain.

"You the Incredible Hulk or something?" I gasped. "Werewolf? Troll with glamour? Elephant shifter?"

He didn't reply; instead, he ran a hand over my legs, carefully easing my hips around. One hand came under my ass, the other across my shoulders.

This was going to hurt.

I blacked out as he pulled me from the car, only to come to with him carrying me snug against a rock-hard body, his hands gentle as they cradled me and supported my injured leg. I could feel the wiry softness of his beard against my face, feel the strength in his muscular arms. This would have been an amazing romance novel if only I wasn't in so much pain.

The next thing I knew, he was nudging a door open with his foot and carrying me into a one-room log cabin. A cheerful fire crackled in a stone fireplace against one wall. There was a pair of rough-hewn chairs and a table, a set of shelves with cooking utensils, and in the corner, a bed which seemed to be covered with a weird combination of cheap fleece blankets, leather, and animal skins.

Kinky. Or survivalist Grizzly Adams. Or kinky survivalist Grizzly Adams.

A chattering noise filled the room and a raccoon jumped onto the table, rising on its two hind legs to wave front paws in the air. It had to have been one of the biggest, fattest raccoons I'd ever seen in my life.

"She returned," the man told the raccoon. "And once I am free, you will get your reward. I keep my vows."

Okay, so hot Grizzly Adams here had a pet raccoon. Given that I'd been contemplating a cat or possibly a dog adoption in my near future, I wasn't about to point fingers. People who lived alone...well, got lonely. I certainly knew that.

"What's his name?" I gasped, inclining my head toward the raccoon. It clearly says a lot about my mental, emotional, and physical state that I was asking the raccoon's name and not the name of this gorgeous man carrying me.

"Diebin."

Cute. I hoped he didn't bite. I shifted a bit in the man's arms and winced.

"You okay?" he asked.

"I'll live." My breath was warm against his beard. I thought I'd live anyway. Cuts. Bruises. My rib. My left leg. Hopefully that was it and the adrenaline wasn't covering up a ruptured spleen or a brain bleed or anything.

"Thanks for finding me and getting me out of the truck," I added, wondering why he was still standing in the middle of the room with me in his arms. Not that I was complaining or anything. I mean, a hot guy holding me was pretty darned nice. And I was certain the act of setting me down somewhere was going to bring on a fresh wave of agony.

"I serve in the hope that you'll finally free me," he announced.

Free him? What the hell was he talking about? Was he a shifter chafing under the rules of his pack? Was he under some sort of indentured servitude to the fae? A nine-to-five desk job he just couldn't take any more?

"I'll do all I can," I told him. The least I could do for this guy was get him out of whatever entanglement he needed freeing from, but even in my hurt state, I knew better than to blindly promise something I might not be able to deliver on. As a Perkins, I had significant standing in Accident, but there were things the family name couldn't overcome. And compared to Cassie, I wasn't all that powerful a witch. I could enchant objects—especially metal objects—but big spells took time as well as the appropriate astrological conditions. I wasn't gifted enough to do much magic on the fly as some of my sisters could.

"Why have you not healed yourself?" He eyed my leg. "Did your flying vehicle spell fail? Has another witch cursed you and blocked your powers?"

I blinked, surprised that he knew I was a witch. I mean, if he went into town or up to the wolf pack compound, then he would obviously have heard about the Perkins sisters and how we were witches descended from the town founder. Someone might have pointed me out to him. But why didn't I know him? I made it a habit to know all the town residents. How had this guy slipped in without my seeing him? Because someone who looked like he did wasn't someone I'd see and forget.

"I can't do flying spells. And I haven't been cursed—just a storm and a mechanical issue and a rockslide." I grimaced, remembering the feeling of my truck going off the mountain. "And I suck at healing. That's Glenda. My skill is in enchanting objects. Besides that, right now I'm in too much pain to concentrate. No magic happening here. Not at the moment."

Whew. Saying all that had completely worn me out. The kinky leather-and-fur bed was looking mighty inviting. Of course, just being here in these guy's arms was pretty darn sweet as well.

He chuckled. "I am not skilled in healing, either. My talents lay in a very different direction."

As much pain as I was in, my mind went right to the gutter. Talents. A guy that looked like this... damn, broken leg or not, I was not going to refuse if he offered up those sorts of talents to me.

"I've seen enough injuries in my life that I know how to set bones and check for bleeding," he added.

As grateful as I was that my savior knew basic first aid, I got the feeling I might need more than splints and bandages. "Got a phone? Can you call an ambulance? Get Ophelia. Tell Cassie. Cassie needs to know. She'll worry. Don't want her to worry."

Shit, I was totally rambling. Going off the rails here. I'd already plunged over the side of a cliff physically, and now it seemed my mind was doing the same thing.

The man didn't answer me; instead, he crossed the room and laid me gently on the bed. Then he walked over to pick up what looked to be an old hunting knife with a rawhide handle from the table with the raccoon on it. I stared at the knife, thinking how amazing it would be in ritual. I could imbue such an object with magic, enchant it, and I got the impression that this knife would be the perfect medium to hold a spell.

It was also perfect for cutting my clothes off.

"Hey!" The knife sliced right through my tank top before I had a chance to get the word out. Darn it, that was one of my favorite tank tops, too.

"I need to check your injuries," he told me.

I looked down, thinking that he was probably going to have to cut my pants off, but that my shirt could have stayed on. That's when I realized I had a huge diagonal bruise across my chest, some raw and red seatbelt burns, and that the tank top

31

was most likely a goner even before he'd started cutting. Even if I could get the blood out of it, there were holes and a rip right across where the bottom of my boob had been. Yeah, the shirt probably needed to go. The guy knew first aid. I was probably in shock. I needed to shut up and just let him do his thing.

Trust. It wasn't something I gave easily, but something told me I could trust this man.

"Okay. Sorry. Go ahead."

I grimaced as he continued to slice with the knife, but I didn't protest further. I tended to be more modest than most of my sisters, but it wasn't like anyone had ever cared about seeing my naked body before, so I wasn't particularly shy about this guy hacking the tank top from my body. He eased the scraps from under me and tossed them to the floor, his gaze roaming across my skin.

It sent goosebumps in a wave over my flesh. Plenty of doctors and nurses had given my body a clinical once-over in my life, but there was something about the way this man looked at me. It was as if what he saw stirred him in some emotional way.

It was as if he wanted to do more than just look.

Before I realized what was happening, he moved to cut my bra off.

"Oh, no. Not that." I wrapped my hands across my boobs, not wanting to go that far.

"You're hurt." He traced the bruise and rash from the seat-belt with the hand not holding the knife.

"The ta-tas are fine. You can clean around the bra. Or put salve around the bra."

"Let me check."

I considered the request and thought about what was left of my pride, then removed my hands from my breasts. "Okay. Just leave the bra on."

He rolled his eyes, then gently eased the front of my bra

down just enough to see the mark from the seatbelt. Gentle fingers traced the mark, then caressed the curve of my breasts before moving to cup them, brushing a thumb across my nipple. I sucked in a breath, immediately thinking of what those fingers could be doing elsewhere.

With a lingering glance, his hands left my breasts and he got to work on removing my jeans, which quickly wiped out any sexy-time thoughts from my mind. Oh. My. God. Every slice of fabric, every slight move of my leg sent a fresh wave of agony through me.

"It's broken."

"Yeah. No, shit," I panted. "Both? Or just the left one?"

"Left. Your knee is swollen on the right, and there's a deep bruise on your thigh where you were pinned by that metal. Left leg has the break. Luckily, it's incomplete."

Incomplete. My sister Ophelia was a paramedic and I knew enough to realize that meant that the bone hadn't completely severed in two. It wasn't sticking through my leg. It was still broken, but not two dangling pieces under my skin. It meant I didn't need surgery, that all I needed was a cast for it to heal.

I should have been relieved, but I wasn't.

Damn it. Tears burned my eyes at the thought that I'd be immobilized probably for months. How bad was my knee on the right leg? And that bruise...was that the sort of thing that would cause blood clots? All those late-night WebMD searches flooded my brain and I began to panic.

"No, my witch." He smoothed my hair, his voice like hot chocolate on a winter day. "Don't cry. I will take care of you. I will help you and care for you now and always. You've returned and I am yours. I yield to you. I will obey any request you make of me. And I won't let you lie in pain. I can't heal, but together we can work great magic."

Huh? Was this some sort of auditory hallucination? The

pain *was* lessening in both my leg and my chest, but was that the effect of severed nerves? Me going into shock? Or was it that a totally hot guy had just announced he was mine and was yielding to me, and broken bones suddenly weren't all that important by comparison?

The man covered me with a fleecy blanket that had a scene from The Lion King on it and some of the furs, then stepped away for a few minutes, returning with two pieces of wood and a few rags. He set them down, then gently ran his fingers over the skin of my left leg, pausing where I assumed the break was. I didn't know if it was something magical he was doing, or if it was the incredible sensation of his touch, but the pain subsided, a strange numbness taking its place.

"I will put a splint on your leg to help immobilize it and help with healing and the pain," he informed me. "But first, let's put some ice packs on your knee and that bruise."

"Are my ribs broken?" I asked as he picked up one of two plastic gel packs, breaking and kneading it to activate the chemicals.

"No, I think the muscles are bruised from whatever was across your chest." He placed one ice pack on my right knee, then started activating the other one. "I believe I have some antibiotic salve that might help with the scrapes, though."

The man was like a regular pharmacy. I guess if I lived on the side of a mountain, I'd want to have all the bases covered as well as have a solid supply of first-aid products. It's not like he could quickly pop into town and grab some aspirin and cough medicine.

Which reminded me.

"You wouldn't have any Tylenol or anything, would you?"

He nodded, putting the second ice pack on my bruise, then heading over toward the book shelves. When returned, he had two pills and a cup of water. I took them gratefully, then closed my eyes as he began to splint my leg.

It hurt. No amount of hot-guy-feeling-up-my-leg vibes could disguise the fact that every gentle movement sent a stab of pain through me.

"There. All done."

I opened my eyes to see what looked to my untutored eyes to be a very professional splint. My leg was truly immobilized, held straight by the wood and the cloth.

"How'd you know how to do that?" I asked.

"I've witnessed many human conflicts." He turned away and went to the fire, pouring steaming water from a pot into a bowl. "This is my first time putting what I've seen into practice though, so I hope I've done it correctly."

He brought the bowl over beside the bed and got some soap and a washcloth. Then he headed back to the fire, pouring more of the steaming water into a mug and adding a tea bag.

"Here. Drink this, and I will wash you up and apply some of the ointment to your wounds."

I sipped the tea, which according to the tag was Sleepytime chamomile, as the man removed my blankets, dipped the washcloth into the steaming water, and began to gently wipe the blood from my skin. It was downright erotic. And I fully realized how sad my love life was that having a man clean blood off my bruised and cut skin was the hottest thing that had ever happened to me in my life.

He clucked over the scrapes from the seatbelt, cleaning, drying, then smoothing ointment over the raw skin. I tried to cover up my reaction to his touch by sipping the tea, but there was nothing I could do about the way my breath hitched every time he touched me, or that my hardened nipples were clearly visible through my thin bra fabric. It was embarrassing. It was even more embarrassing because he noticed.

"If only you were not hurt, my witch." He rubbed across

one of my nipples with his thumb, fanning his fingers out to trace along the top of my breast. Everything tightened inside, heat settling into my core.

"Yeah." My voice was breathy. "Maybe later, when I'm not so banged up?"

Who was I kidding? Guys were never into me. Guys this hot were *definitely* never into me. Whatever this was, it was fleeting and by the time I wasn't feeling like I'd been tossed down the side of a mountain, it would be gone. And so would he. Gone. Uninterested. Just friends. The usual.

"I'm not sure I can wait that long, my witch."

Me, neither. I was starting to wonder how many Tylenol I'd need to take to make sex with a broken leg enjoyable. Probably the whole bottle.

"Soon." He smiled, covered me up with an entire zoo of fur pelts, then took the basin of water over to the table while I drank my tea and tried to get my libido in check.

Then he put a cassette tape into a boom box that looked like it was straight out of the eighties. A sound poured from the speakers—Steely Dan. I settled into the soft blanket and furs, listening to the music as he brought me more tea. By the time I was done with the second cup of tea, I was happily on the edge of sleep, listening to *Hey Nineteen*.

"Thank you," I whispered, my eyelids drifting shut. "I can't thank you enough for what you've done for me."

"I am yours, Adelaide," the man replied. "Yours. You've returned to set me free, and I will serve you for all eternity."

I floated to sleep, a tiny bit concerned that I'd just somehow attracted a very sexy stalker and wondering who the heck was Adelaide.

CHAPTER 5

BRONWYN

I woke to the smell of stew and Diebin staring at me from the edge of my bed. My first thought was that I hoped the raccoon wasn't rabid, because damn it all, a broken leg was bad enough. My second thought was that whatever that was cooking on the fire, I wanted it in my belly right now.

Not wanting to attempt hopping my way over to the food, I put out a tentative hand, wondering if Diebin was friendly.

The raccoon stared at my fingers and made a chattering noise. Then he gave me the equivalent of a high five. A paw five? Either way, I'd take it as a positive sign that this guy wasn't harboring secret plans of mauling me.

"How are you feeling?" a deep voice asked.

I shifted around to look at the man, immediately regretting the action. "Sore. Bruised. I feel better, but I'm pretty sure I'm not going to be dancing the jig any time soon."

"If you're up to it, then you should eat."

He approached and bent to wrap his arms around me, gently easing me into a sitting position. I rode out the pain, fully aware that I was wearing nothing but a bra and panties, and that his efforts put his head right against my breasts. Soft beard and hair. Warm breath against my skin. Muscular arms around me that looked like they belonged to a lumberjack.

All too soon I was sitting upright, a folded fur supporting my leg. The man had his back to me, stirring the stew, so I took the opportunity to check out his medical handiwork and my injuries. The diagonal red mark and bruise from my left shoulder to my right hip had definitely improved. I was glad the seatbelt had done its job or I would have been bounced around the inside of my truck like a freaking ping pong ball. The bruise on my left thigh was huge and dark, but it didn't look like something that would cost me my life by my inexpert estimation. My right knee was still a little swollen, but a few tentative tries told me that I could bend it. Good. One leg working was better than none. I couldn't see what was going on under the splint on my lower left leg, but from the steady throbbing, I knew this was my most serious injury.

I'd take it. Thank heaven for seatbelts and airbags. I'd gone over the side of a mountain. I could have died. I could have had internal injuries or split my head open, or had my legs smashed into little fragments. I was so lucky to have survived this with what truly were minor injuries. And I was so lucky that this hottie had been living near where I'd crashed and been home to help me.

The man returned with two bowls of the stew, dragging a chair over beside the bed with one of his feet. He handed me a bowl, then sat beside me, the second one on his lap. Diebin chattered, then hopped off the bed to head to another bowl on the floor by the table. We ate in silence. And damn if this wasn't the best thing I'd ever eaten in my life—and that included food my sister Glenda had cooked. I think it had to do with being in the woods, hungry, and having had a near-death experience. Somehow all that made this plain stew like manna from heaven.

My companion ate in silence, every now and then glancing up to check on me, his eyes roving over my exposed skin. It was making me uncomfortable—and not necessarily in a bad way, either.

"What's your name?" I asked him. Crap, I knew the raccoon's name but not his. I was a horrible excuse for a damsel in distress.

"Hadur."

That was it. No last name. No elaboration. Personally, I liked a man of few words, not that I had all that much experience with men outside of a professional or friendship capacity. This made conversation a bit one-sided though.

"Are you part of the pack, Hadur?" I asked, realizing that the answer was probably "no." Up until recently, Dallas' werewolf pack didn't allow for lone wolves. You were either in the pack or you were dead. And I didn't get the impression that this guy was a newly separated member of the pack. He'd been out here in the woods a long time—a very long time, from my estimation.

"The werewolves?" He fingered one of the pelts on the bed. "They know to stay away."

Ewww. I was going to pretend that these furs covering me were animal-animals. Pretending hard, here—very hard.

"So what kind of shifter are you? Bear?" He seemed like a bear with his powerful body and his loner lifestyle.

He shot me a puzzled glance. "No. I'm yours."

"My what?" I pressed. "Don't get me wrong, I'm super grateful you came along when you did and got me out of that truck. I'm grateful for you taking care of me and feeding me this amazing stew, which I really really hope isn't werewolf or at least a werewolf that I know personally. I don't want to pry or anything, but you're clearly not human if you're

39

ripping doors off a wrecked truck and bending dashboards. So, shifter? Incredible Hulk? Jason Momoa bitten by a radioactive spider?"

"I am a demon of war—your demon. I've waited for you to come back. I yield to you and will do as you bid of me, my witch. I have waited so long. I feared you would never return, but you've finally returned. And I will be yours. I will do whatever you command. I will serve you for all eternity."

Oh, God, this was quite possibly the most erotic thing I'd ever experienced—not that I'd ever experienced anything remotely erotic in my thirty-one years of life. Why, oh why did this have to happen when I was immobilized in bed with a broken leg? Why?

"So…a demon." The only experience I'd had with demons was Lucien, the guy Cassie was shacked up with. He was hot, sexy, dangerous, not the sort of individual I'd expect to be living out in the woods all by himself. Clearly this guy was different.

And he'd said a war demon. That sent up all sorts of red flags in my mind, although he didn't seem particularly violent or angry or anything sitting here next to me with an empty bowl of stew in his lap.

"Why are you here, Hadur?" I waved a hand around at the cabin. "How long have you been living out here in the woods by yourself?"

He tilted his head. "I've been here since I was summoned. I cannot leave until I am released."

A lump settled in my stomach that had nothing to do with the stew I'd just eaten. "How long? How long has it been since you've been summoned?"

"Two hundred years? Possibly a decade or two more. I've lost track of time out here." He reached out a finger to trace the line of my jaw, then brushed across my lower lip. "I thought…I thought you would never return. When I felt your presence, felt you cross the boundaries, I could hardly believe it. You are here. You have returned, and I will do all you ask, my witch. I will serve you, Adelaide."

This was better than those romance novels. This was better than a porno. This was way better than that vibrator in my bedside table, and the guy hadn't even kissed me. Had I died and gone to heaven? Because I might totally be okay with that if my leg suddenly miraculously healed and this guy started serving me and doing as I asked.

Wait, who was Adelaide?

"I'm Bronwyn Perkins, not Adelaide." I held out my hand, the one not holding the empty stew bowl. "Not sure if that makes a difference or not on you serving me. Although that sort of thing might need to wait until my leg heals. If you're still interested. Because if you're not, that's okay. It's not like anyone else is. Interested, that is."

Crap. I needed to just shut up. I was making a huge fool out of myself. The guy hadn't made any move to shake my hand, so I let it fall onto the pelt-that-I-hoped-wasn't-werewolf.

"Bronwyn Perkins?" He shook his head, a bemused expression on his face. "Of course. Humans do not live for very long, at least those not bonded to a demon. Two hundred years would be too long for Adelaide to still be alive. So, you are…"

"Probably a great, great, great, grand-niece or something, if Adelaide's last name was Perkins," I told him. "Is she the one who summoned you?"

I suddenly had a whole romantic tragedy running through my head of a young woman in a dress and corset, summoning a demon out in the woods and vowing to come back, only to get run over by a wagon or hit by a falling tree before she could return. And here the demon sat, for two hundred years, pining for his lost…summoner.

Okay, I clearly had been reading too many novels. That, and the fact that the only demon I'd ever met was bumping uglies with my sister, made me assume Hadur and Adelaide were some kind of Romeo and Juliet. For all I knew, Adelaide was a wart-nosed ninety-year-old witch who'd summoned Hadur with murder on her mind and had stroked out before being able to release him from the circle and send him off to kill whoever she felt needed killing.

"I had believed Adelaide was the witch who brought me from hell. I was summoned, and when I appeared, she was the only witch present. But she claimed that she had not been the one to summon me. She demanded I reply to questions I did not know the answer to, then left, vowing to come back. I never saw her again."

Yep. Definitely Romeo and Juliet, even if Adelaide had been ninety and wart-nosed. Hey, elderly disfigured witches deserved love, too.

"So, you've been here alone for two hundred years, give or take a few decades?"

For a brief second, he smiled, and I realized that was the first time I'd seen him do so.

"Yes. Alone aside from Diebin and other beings of the forest."

"Werewolves?" I stroked the pelt with tentative fingers.

"Just the one. They don't come to this section of the mountain. They believe there is evil here." Again with the brief smile. "They are right."

"And you killed the werewolf?"

He shrugged. "The werewolf was very disagreeable."

Okay, I kinda understood that. The werewolves were on the whole a disagreeable bunch. And if he were to be trapped here for hundreds of years, alone, I could see he might be a bit pissed at having some jackwad come into his home and be a total asshole. Still...

"So how big is this circle you're trapped in?" I mentally tried to calculate the distance from my wrecked truck to this cabin. It wasn't easy since it had been raining and I'd been in pain, and he'd been carrying me.

"The circle diameter is approximately two hundred feet."

I blinked. That was less than three quarters of an acre. Admittedly, there were prison cells smaller than that, but to be cooped up in such a small area for over two hundred years...

"You built the house? And—" I glanced at the pot over the fire—"smelted iron? On less than an acre?"

"I did build the house and some of the furniture. I also hunt animals who venture into the confines of the circle. Diebin has provided the other items for me."

I eyed the raccoon. Yeah, he was a big boy, but how the hell had he managed to drag a heavy iron pot through the woods? Guess I never should underestimate the thievery skills and strength of a raccoon.

"Diebin...is he some sort of familiar?"

"That's probably the closest term for what our relation-ship is. We have a partnership. I have granted him eternal life, enhanced strength, speed, and understanding, and he serves me."

I wasn't going to delve into how similar that sounded to the relationship he was pledging to me. Cassie had told me Lucien could extend her life, provide immortality. That was one of the benefits of a witch bonding with a demon—that and enhanced magical ability. But I assumed there had to be more. I assumed that there needed to be a connection between the witch and demon, not just a swipe-right if you think he's cute thing. Cassie and Lucien...well, it was still pretty early in their relationship, but they were obviously in love.

I'd totally do this guy, but no matter how hot he was, I

wasn't going to jump into a "I'll serve you forever" thing with both feet.

"My sister Adrienne talks to animals." I looked around at all the items in the cabin that Diebin must have pilfered from town. No doubt ninety percent of our theft problem could be laid at this guy's paws. "She can call animals to her, get them to do her bidding, communicate with them. It makes all the shifters in town super nervous, because their animal side is susceptible to her influence."

Adrienne spent more time outside of Accident then she did inside, probably for those very reasons. Every now and then someone would call her to take care of the non-vampire bats in their attic, or a wasp nest in their eaves, but most of her pest and wildlife removal customers tended to be outside of the town wards.

"She is a witch as well?"

I nodded. "We're all witches. Seven sisters."

Diebin let out a stream of chatter.

"He says he knows your sister. She has convinced him to vacate several homes and a chicken coop." Hadur scowled. "That's why we do not have more chicken for dinner."

"Sorry?" I squeaked, thinking that the guy looked really intimidating when he scowled. Kind of a combination of scary and hot.

"No matter. Diebin has other options when it comes to providing me what I need. A few years ago, he discovered a large building filled with food and household goods."

Shit, the raccoon was probably raiding the new Walmart that had opened in the town just over from Accident. I ran my hand across the cotton sheets under the pelts and took note of candles, dishes, silverware, even a few books stacked up on the table. Paperbacks. Stephen King. Huh. No surprise there.

"I'll get you some more tea, and you rest. When you wake

up, we'll talk more." Hadur stood and made his way over to a mismatched set of mugs with quirky sayings, selecting a Keep Calm and Slay Your Enemies one. He dropped a teabag in and poured steaming water from a bright blue saucepan.

Less than an acre. For two hundred years. A war demon. Shit, I felt so bad for this guy. Even though he didn't seem to have been driven mad by his captivity, the way in which he'd eagerly pledged himself to me told me he was desperate to be free of his confines.

And I *was* going to free him. As soon as I could walk again. Which might be a while. I suddenly envisioned myself trying to hop through the forest and up the side of a mountain with a broken leg and the reality of my situation came crashing down on me.

Judging from the faint light outside the one window, it was early morning the day after I'd left the werewolf compound. Had anyone realized I was missing yet? Probably not. There was a good chance no one would know I was gone until I didn't show up at the family dinner on Sunday at Cassie's house. Maybe if one of my sisters called me for something and I didn't respond, but that still might be days before they sent up an alarm.

I hated the thought of them worrying about me, but even more, I was filled with self-pity at the realization that no one would miss me for days. No one. Not even a cat or a dog. I actually envied Hadur his raccoon buddy. I didn't even have that.

"My sisters are probably going to eventually come looking for me," I told the demon. "Is there some way I can get a message to them? A flare? Smoke signals? A cell phone?" *A cell phone.* "Actually, can you go back to my truck and find my cell phone?"

The raccoon chattered and hopped off the table, dashing through something that looked suspiciously like a doggie door, while Hadur brought me a hot cup of tea. "Diebin will find your belongings. But in the meantime, you must rest and heal."

I drank the tea, feeling immediately drowsy, the pain in my leg reduced to a dull throb. Nice tea. Nice stew. I'd sleep for a bit. And hopefully when I woke up, Diebin would be back with my cell phone.

CHAPTER 6

BRONWYN

*D*iebin had brought just about everything from my
smashed truck *except* my cell phone. I now had my
purse and wallet, lipstick, a handkerchief, my keys, and my
favorite pair of nippers.

Don't judge. I was especially thrilled to see my nippers. I
owned four sets, but these were the best ones and I really
didn't want to lose them. I'd been envisioning my tools scattered down the side of a mountain, my little trailer
destroyed, my forge smashed beyond repair. Yes, tools can be
replaced, but those tools that fit your hand just right and
seemed to be formed just right are irreplaceable. You can buy
twenty pairs of nippers, but you'll never find that exactly
perfect one ever again.

Oh, no. My forge. My trailer. Destroyed. Gone.

I cried thinking of my truck and the tools of my trade,
forever ruined, broken and flung across the side of a mountain as we'd tumbled off that cliff. I was lucky to be alive, but
here I was crying about my trailer and my tools.

Hadur didn't seem to know what to make of my tears. He
kept offering me more tea and sending Diebin back to my

wrecked truck for whatever the raccoon could find. Eventually he did bring my cell phone, which had all of ten percent battery left. It didn't matter. The cell signal down here in this cabin was nonexistent. If I didn't have a broken leg, I probably could have climbed up somewhere and gotten a signal, but *I had a broken leg*. And Hadur couldn't go outside of the perimeter of his summoning circle. And Diebin couldn't operate a cell phone, let alone talk to anyone. Except perhaps Adrienne.

I wondered if Adrienne could understand animals over the phone, or was that just in person? I'd need to ask her once I got back home. Perhaps we could do an experiment where I called her from an animal shelter to see if she could communicate with the cats and dogs there via phone. *When* I got back home. Which didn't look to be any time soon.

And there was another problem besides my being surrounded by random items from my truck and holding a non-functional cell phone. A serious problem. I problem I didn't quite know how to solve. All the tea Hadur had been giving me made me need to pee.

There was clearly no bathroom in this cabin. Even if there was, I wasn't sure I could get out of bed and hobble to one. Crutches? A bed pan? I needed to come up with a solution soon, or I was going to be wetting the bed, and that was a far more humiliating option then having this sexy demon help me pee in a frying pan.

"I need to get out of the bed," I told Hadur.

He frowned down at my leg. "You have not healed yourself yet."

"I know, but I'll need to be up and moving around long before that bone heals. Can you put together some makeshift crutches? Long pieces of wood with a cross piece at top to go under my arms? They'll steady my weight on the one leg so I can move around."

He grumbled something under his breath about not understanding witches, then picked up a knife and an axe. "Stay in bed. Rest. I'll be back with these crutches."

I waited until he and the raccoon had left, then immediately tried to get out of bed. My right foot hit the floor, my knee stiff but cooperating. Then I tried to ease my left leg along the bed and onto the ground, hoping the splint and bandage thing the demon had put together kept my leg immobile.

I'm not gonna lie, it hurt like hell, but I didn't feel like the broken bone was shifting or anything. Holding onto the bedpost, I slowly stood, keeping my weight on the right leg—the right leg with the bum knee.

This was insane. I stood, gripping the bedpost firmly, knowing that if my knee gave out, I was going down and that was going to be really, really bad. I was up, but that was the least of the challenges I'd face trying to take care of my bathroom needs. First, how the heck was I going to cross the room to get outside to pee? Secondly, I was still wearing my underwear. Scooting them down and squatting to relieve myself was most likely going to be beyond my athletic skills at the moment.

Take the underwear off? Pee, then somehow manage to get them back on? Or say screw the underwear and just be commando until someone came to rescue me? It's not like this guy seeing an extra few inches of flesh was gonna send him over the edge. Perhaps Diebin could run into Walmart and get me some spare clothing. Maybe Hadur had an extra t-shirt around I could wear—one that was long enough to cover my naked ass.

I decided I should tackle one problem at a time, so I used the hand that wasn't holding onto the bedpost for dear life to scoot down my underwear past my knees, then eased myself down on the bed and pulled my right leg out of them.

Step one—no underwear. Although having them dangle off the makeshift splint wasn't the most dignified thing in the world, it would have to do. I got myself upright again and eyed the distance between the bed and the door.

I was so not going to make that. Was there a bowl or something I could use as a bedpan? A roll of paper towels I could stack up to pee on? Why the heck couldn't this demon have indoor plumbing, or have his raccoon steal a camp toilet from somewhere? Frying pan or door. Frying pan or door. I needed to make a decision soon or I was going to be peeing right here by the bed.

Door. I might be stupid, but I couldn't stand the thought of peeing in a pan that was most likely going to be used to prepare my dinner.

The path to the door was long and torturous because I didn't have crutches and couldn't hop my way across the room. Instead I had to hug the walls and scant furniture, making my way a few tiny inches at a time. Each shuffle forward jolted my left leg and sent a fresh wave of pain through me. By the time I reached the door, I was panting and sweaty. At least I hoped that was sweat and not pee trickling down my leg.

The door didn't have a knob or anything conventional in the way of an opening device—just a leather strap. I grabbed it and tugged, not realizing the door was quite so heavy or that something installed by a demon in the woods without a licensed homebuilder to assist might not open smoothly and evenly. I pulled. It resisted, then flung open. I teetered, lost my balance, and fell to the floor.

Thankfully I'd landed on my right side. Although I jarred my splinted leg enough that I cried out from the pain. I probably peed. Just a little. I was going to pretend it was sweat.

I lay there on the ground, which gave me a clear view of the books and magazines stacked next to the table. Popular

Mechanics. G.Q. Tiger Beat. I guess if you've got a raccoon in charge of providing your reading selection, you're gonna get the occasional Tiger Beat. The books were just as eclectic. One on decorative mosaic containers. The Stephen King books I'd seen from the bed. A couple of Patterson thrillers. Gone Girl. Little Women. The Fifty Shades books.

Hadur burst through the open doorway, stopping and staring down at me.

"What…what happened?"

"I'm not into that stuff." I pointed to the Fifty Shades books. "Just thought you should know." Not that the demon was probably thinking sexy-times with me sprawled across the floor in my own pee. Just a little pee. Probably sweat.

"You screamed."

"It wasn't really a scream. More of a shout. A quiet shout. Okay, yes, I screamed."

"What happened?"

God, I had to pee so bad. So very bad. I was already pretty much naked on the floor, lying in just a little bit of sweat. How much more embarrassing could it all get?

"I had to pee and tried to make it outside, but I fell. And this is sweat, you know. Sweat. Because hobbling around the room with a broken leg worked up quite a sweat."

"I would have helped you. Why didn't you wait?"

"Well, help me now," I snapped. "Less talk and more helping before there's more sweat on your floor."

That got him moving. Once more I was gently scooped up in a demon's arms, concentrating very hard on bladder control as Hadur carried me outside and a few feet away from the house. He eased me down, supporting me under my arms as I did an awkward squat.

Annnnd nothing.

My bladder screamed for release, but I just couldn't do it.

"You said you had to urinate?"

51

"Yes, I said that."

"Then why—"

"Stage fright," I snapped. "Can you just lean me against a tree and give me a branch to hold for balance, then go around to the other side of the cabin?"

He huffed out a breath, muttered something about "witches," then picked me up again, propping me against a tree and handing me two branches. I waited until he vanished inside the cabin, then carefully widened my stance, scooting my back painfully down the bark of the tree.

Blessed relief. There were some logistical concerns involving the flow of liquid on the ground and whether the widening puddle might reach my feet or not. Oh, and the lack of toilet paper. I did the hip shake, which was pretty ineffectual given that I had a broken leg and was squatting against a tree trunk, balancing myself with two rather thin branches.

Done, I wiggled myself back into a standing position, grimacing to think of how much bark was probably embedded in my back. Crap. I hoped this tree didn't have poison oak on it or something.

"I'm done!" I called out.

It took Hadur a few minutes to exit the cabin. It gave me time to contemplate the fact that I was naked except for my bra, with my panties still stuck like some lewd accessory on my leg splint. Naked. Sweaty—it was sweat, I swear it was sweat. I was probably going to have to go through this all over again in another few hours. Oh, no. What if I had to number two? How the hell was that going to work? I mean, I knew how it was going to work, just not how it was going to work and leave me with any dignity whatsoever.

I sent up a quick prayer for constipation.

It figured. The hottest guy I'd ever seen, and me mostly naked, and I was gonna blow it because of a broken leg and biological necessities. I needed to get out of here. I needed my sisters to come rescue me and take me home where I could get a proper cast and crutches and a flush toilet. And then I could come back after I was all healed wearing something sexy and maybe bringing food that wasn't stolen out of a Walmart and make a better impression on this hot demon guy.

Hadur appeared, walked over and scooped me up, and carried me inside where he sat me down on a chair and promptly cut the underwear off my leg.

"I cleaned the sweat off the floor." There was a whole lot of humor in his voice and I wasn't sure if I liked that or not. I mean, I guess it was good that he found the whole thing funny and wasn't upset that I'd sweated a little on his floor, but the whole event was one more negative check mark in the is-Bronwyn-ever-going-to-get-laid tally.

"Thank you," I replied. "Do you have anything I could possibly wear? Like a super long t-shirt? I promise I'll be careful not to get any sweat on it when I need to sweat in the future."

"I like you naked."

Well, that was a first. "So, you like six-foot-tall women with linebacker figures, sweat in places I don't want to mention, bruises and scrapes, a broken leg, and probably poison ivy down their backs?"

He ran a hand up my bicep. "You're strong in the right places…" The hand skimmed across the curve of my small breasts then down to my not-so-flat belly. "And soft in the right places. As for the rest, that just gives me an excuse to bathe you."

Bathe? I turned to the side and noticed what looked like a shallow black rubber feed trough full of steaming water.

"How'd you get the water hot?" I asked, calculating the time it would take to boil all that over a fire. "Did Diebin steal you a hot water heater? And a propane tank? Hey!" I swatted at his hands as he went to remove my bra. I know, it was a bit ridiculous to be modest about showing my boobs when my happy-spot was right there on display.

"Humans no longer bathe naked? I assumed from some of the magazines Diebin brought me that modern humans, especially women, spent a great deal of their time naked."

Seems Diebin had occasionally brought him something racier than Tiger Beat. "We do bathe naked, It's just…." This was stupid. The guy had seen everything else. It wasn't like removing a few inches of silk and lace was going to make much of a difference. "Okay. Just don't cut the bra off. I like this one. There's hooks in the back."

I was perfectly capable of unhooking my own bra, but before I could tell him that, he'd reached around me, struggling a little with the tiny hooks. It put him against me, warm, strong, masculine. My face was right in line with his shoulder, and I leaned forward just enough to brush his skin with my lips.

The bra came free. Hadur pulled away, taking the undergarment with him as I eased my arms out of the straps. He draped the bra across the back of a chair, then turned to me, his eyes on my breasts. I took a breath, feeling my nipples harden at his gaze.

Yep. It was just like one of those books. Well, not the Fifty Shades ones, but the others that didn't involve getting smacked with a riding crop and tied up.

He reached out and brushed his fingers across my nipples, lightly tracing the curve of my breasts before pulling his hand away. We stood there—well, he stood and I sat—and all I could think of was broken leg or not, I wanted this man, this demon, to take this whole thing across the finish line.

After a bath, that is. Because I was dirty, and…sweaty. Yeah, sweaty.

I reached out to steady myself on his arm, then carefully rose to my feet, grateful that all those Pilates DVDs had given me some decent core body strength under my soft belly. He went to pick me up, and I waved his hand away, using him instead to help me hobble over to the trough-tub. Once there, I had to let him scoop me up and deposit me into the water, my broken leg raised and cushioned on some towels over the edge of the trough.

"Am I supposed to get this wet?" I motioned to the splint.

"If it gets wet, I will rebandage it with dry cloth," he assured me.

I grimaced, thinking how badly *that* was going to hurt. I really needed a cast. I really needed to get out of here and get some actual medical attention. But the reality was that unless Diebin was smart enough to track down Adrienne, it would probably be another two or three days before I was rescued.

In the meantime, I was in a steamy hot bath complete with a washcloth and some very nice smelling soap. I reached for the washcloth only to have him move it from my grasp.

"No. That's my job. You relax, and I'll wash you."

Holy cow, he was going to wash me. I'd never had anyone else wash me in my life. Well, aside from when I was a baby, I supposed. I watched him lather up the washcloth and shivered with anticipation. Then I did as he said. I leaned my head back, closed my eyes, and relaxed.

I could hear the crackle of the fire, the splash of the water. I could feel the rough washcloth on my shoulders, down my arms, across my back and chest. I shivered slightly as the washcloth left my body to dunk into the water. Then it returned, rinsing off the suds. The second time I heard the splash of the water, it was his hands on my breasts as the washcloth brushed across my hip and down my right leg.

Fingers rolled one of my nipples and I gasped, opening

my eyes to find him watching me. With his eyes on mine, he bent his head and took the other nipple into his mouth.

I suddenly didn't care one bit about my broken leg. Sucking in a breath, I closed my eyes again, concentrating on the feeling of his mouth and hand on my breasts.

"Keep doing that," I gasped.

He scraped his teeth across my nipple. "This? Or this?" Suddenly the washcloth that had been on my legs was gone and I felt his hand moving up my inner thigh.

"Both." I leaned into his touch, feeling his thumb brushing my clit, his palm cupping my sex. I reveled in the sensation of his fingers on and in me, of his mouth on my breast. My world fell away, my body tightening then releasing as an orgasm rolled over me.

His hands soothed me as I rode through the aftershocks. My eyes opened and I watched him watching me.

"That was nice," I told him. Duh. What a stupid thing to say. I should have come up with something sexy, or complimented him on his skill, or told him how I was going to rock his world once my leg healed. Or maybe before. There's no reason I couldn't give him a blow job, well besides the fact that I'd never done one before. I'd seen it in porn. I knew the general gist of the activity. I mean, how hard could it be?

Hard. Har, har, har. Hopefully very hard.

How the heck did I go about telling this guy I wanted to… you know? I wasn't very mobile right now, so it's not like I could just kneel down and go for it. There would need to be some considerable cooperation on his part. This would be a first for me, and I wanted to get it right.

It was *all* a first for me. Yeah, I was that thirty-one-year-old virgin. I know. It sounded so unbelievable in this day and age, like coming across a unicorn. Except we had three unicorns in Accident, so I was actually the rarer. When I was a teen, I was way taller than most of the boys and way stronger than the human ones. It had been easier to pretend disinterest than face rejection, and by the time I'd gotten to college, it was a habit I couldn't break. When I'd reached my mid-twenties, it was just easier to project a vibe that I was unavailable, uninterested. So here I was, a virgin. At thirty-one.

Wait, could I still claim that? I mean, the shaft of love hadn't gotten anywhere close to the cavern of ecstasy, so I guess that technically I still was. But getting off at this demon's hands made me inclined to think otherwise.

Hadur reached out a finger to touch my cheek. "I hope the next time is better than nice. My witch, I can hardly wait until you have healed and I can do all the things to you I'm imagining."

He stood to scoop me out of the tub and I noticed that his pants were looking a bit snug and uncomfortable in a certain area.

"I can...uh, I can help with that," I said as he carried me over to a pile of towels and eased me down onto them. "I mean, I'd like to help with that. Or try to help. Because I'm not all that experienced and might not be that good. Actually, I'm not experienced at all. But I'd like to try."

Sheesh. I was such an idiot. No wonder I was a virgin at thirty-one.

He shot me a puzzled look and started to dry me off. "What are you talking about?"

I felt my face grow even hotter—like ready-to-explode hot. "That." I gestured to the crotch of his pants. "With my hands...or mouth."

He tilted his head, then smiled and bent down to kiss the tip of my nose. "I'm yours, Bronwyn. You don't need to do that. There is no need for you to pleasure me. My job is to serve *you*."

Okay, the sex-slave thing had been intriguingly sexy at first, but it was quickly losing its appeal.

"No. That's not how this is going to work," I told him. "Getting you off makes me feel sexy; it makes me want you more. It brings me just as much pleasure to make you orgasm as it does to have one myself. Well, probably not, but you get the idea. This needs to be mutually beneficial, or it won't work long term."

It still might not work long term, but I'll be damned if I was going to go into my first sexual relationship with this one-sided crap. And to show him that, I reached out and cupped him through his pants.

He hissed and froze, then jerked his hips forward. I rubbed, shifting so I could bring my other hand up to unzip his pants.

"This should wait until your leg heals," he protested as I eased him from his pants. Commando. I liked that in a man…or demon.

"I'm not waiting." I wrapped my hand around him at the base and stroked him to the tip. "Scoot forward a few feet, will you? I can't do this all twisted over on my hip."

He obliged and I sighed in relief once both my ass cheeks were back on the towel. I caressed and stroked him, feeling him harden further. A bead of white swelled at the end of his cock and emboldened by his enthusiastic response, I licked the pearlescent drop. His hips rocked forward and I found him in my mouth.

Huh. That was easier than I'd expected. Imagining myself quite the temptress, I lost myself in the feel of him, in the taste of him. And when he came, I felt more powerful and sexy than I ever had before in my life.

"You need another bath, my witch."

He reached down to trace a finger along my chin, my neck, the top of my breasts. Sticky. I'd not timed things quite right and he'd ended up coming outside of my mouth. It looked sexy in the porn movies, but in reality, it was a bit like being coated in fast-drying hair gel.

"I'll just clean up with a basin of water—" Before I could finish my sentence, he was wiping me up with a warm, wet washcloth.

"Rest," he instructed, scooping me up and placing me back into the bed. "I'll get dinner started. And if you need anything in the future—assistance, food, water, you are to ask me, please. Don't risk hurting your leg further. I will help you."

He turned to go and I reached out and grabbed his hand. I was tired. I did need to sleep. But there was one more thing I wanted.

"Can dinner wait?" I murmured. "I'd really like you to lay here beside me. I want to fall asleep next to you, with your arms around me."

He smiled, and his eyes shown with a golden glow in the light brown irises. "I would like that too, my witch. I would very much like that."

CHAPTER 7

BRONWYN

*T*slept. I slept a lot. I don't know whether it was the hot bath, the orgasm, or just general exhaustion, but I pretty much slept the day away, waking up for dinner and more hot tea, then promptly going right back to sleep.

The next morning, I felt good enough that I made use of a much-needed toothbrush and ultra-whitening toothpaste. Then I hobbled outside with Hadur's assistance and the help of two crutches he'd put together for me while I was sleeping.

And can I just say, Thank God that raccoon brought toilet paper from one of his late-night supply runs.

He'd also brought a carton of fake eggs with chopped up peppers in it, so we ate omelets for breakfast along with some bread that Hadur fried in a pan. After breakfast, I read Tiger Beat and a five-year-old edition of Cosmopolitan, then dozed a bit while Hadur snuggled up against me.

Sleeping with him was the most amazing thing ever. Well, I'm sure sex with him was going to be more amazing then sleeping, but for now the snoozy cuddles were top of my list. Having the security of his solid form behind me, his arm gently around his waist, his warm breath in my hair was pretty darn close to heaven. It wasn't confining; it was comforting. It made me want this private time in his cabin to never end—well, except for the broken leg part.

When I awoke from my nap, Hadur was up and about, another steaming trough of water in the middle of the room, cheese and a selection of crackers on a plate next to my bed. Diebin was nowhere to be found, so I assumed he was out on another run, or off doing whatever raccoons did to entertain themselves. I ate some cheese, drank the tea Hadur had been practically force-feeding me since my arrival, took care of some business out by a tree, and let Hadur help me into the tub.

"You never did tell me how you managed to get this hot water going so quickly." I was fully aware that Hadur was watching me soap up my body. It made everything south of my waist tingle a bit.

"I'm a demon. I can heat water without fire."

"Inside a summoning circle? Because Lucien can't do much of anything inside the town wards beyond show some pretty wings, beat the snot out of werewolves, and juice up Cassie's spells. You're dealing with the effect of the same wards combined with the summoning circle. I'm surprised you can do anything demon-magical at all."

He blinked, shifting his gaze from my boobs to my face. "Lucien?"

"He's my sister Cassie's main squeeze. Do you know him? He's a demon. Says he's Satan's son, but who knows if that's true or not."

"I know Lucien. Why is he here?"

I shrugged, wondering if I could manage to wash my hair or not. Actually, it wasn't the washing I was worried about; it was the conditioning and the combing. My hair was in a short bob, but super fine, and washing it with a bar of rose-scented soap would probably turn it into twelve inches of knotted mess. Hmm. I wonder if Diebin could steal me some dry shampoo from the Walmart?

"I think he told Cassie he was here on vacation. Charon dropped him off or something. He was a bit surprised about the wards around the town. And all the supernatural beings who live here. And the witches."

"Charon brought him." Hadur scowled.

I paused my scrubbing to eye him. "Does that have something to do with you? You said you had no idea who had summoned you or why."

"Most likely not. I was summoned so long ago. And demons cannot summon one another. It was a witch who summoned me."

"And Charon would have no reason to pay a witch to summon you, get you out of his hair or something?" I asked. "Do you demons get into fights? Have feuds?"

He shot me a sideways smile. "I'm a war demon. I get into fights and have feuds all the time. But not with Charon that I remember. He's simply the ferryman. He brings demons into and out of hell that are not summoned."

I nodded, remembering Cassie telling me the dude was like Uber for demons. "But you *were* summoned. Two hundred years ago, you were summoned. And no witch ever showed up to make a request. Why go to all the bother, and I assume it's a big ass bother of a ritual, to summon a demon and not show up to close the deal?"

"I have never known of this happening before," Hadur said. "Never. That is why I was so certain that Adelaide had been the one who summoned me. She was right here at the edge of the circle when I appeared."

"Could she have done it by accident?" I envisioned a witch skipping along, singing some song she'd read in a spell book while just happening to trace the appropriate symbols in the air. The odds of that happening were probably a gazillion to one. And I couldn't see any witch being so stupid as to sing a spell without knowing it might stick. That would be like lighting your drapes on fire then being shocked when they went up in a blaze.

"No. But there might have been another witch nearby."

"You can't tell one witch energy from another?" I asked. Sheesh. Did we really all look alike to demons?

"I can, but families have similar energy. Covens have similar energy." He reached out to touch my shoulder. "When I sensed you, I thought you were Adelaide. Your energy is nearly identical to how I remember hers being."

"We Perkins women," I joked. "Strong family resemblance, I guess." It did make me think of something, though. "Maybe it wasn't Adelaide, but some other member of her family. If it had been a sister of hers, or her mother or an aunt, then you might not have noticed the additional energy and just attributed it all to Adelaide."

He nodded. "Yes, but then why would this other witch not reveal herself, give me my task, and release me from the summoning circle?"

I shrugged. "Maybe this witch wasn't supposed to be summoning demons and didn't want Adelaide to find out? Maybe by the time it was safe for them to come back and give you the task and release you, they'd been struck down with the plague or something?"

The whole thing began to give me a bad feeling. He was a war demon. He stirred up strife and violence and discord. He probably would do that murder-for-hire thing. I was pretty sure demons didn't bat a leathery wing when it came to being summoned to kill. Had one of Adelaide's relatives decided to do away with a few family members or some powerful supernatural residents?

But how would that have worked with the wards around

the town? Lucien could do pretty much nothing inside the town limits. Would a war demon have any power at all in the town? Although I guess lopping off someone's head wouldn't take too much demon power.

The wards. They hadn't always included Heartbreak Mountain. They'd been expanded over the centuries to allow for supernatural residents who didn't want to live in the town proper, and to include what had become the werewolf compound. Maybe at the time of Hadur's summoning, this part of the mountain hadn't been inside the wards. Maybe a witch two hundred years ago had been desperate enough to take care of some threat that she'd turned to demonic help.

But this would remain a mystery until I could get back to town, back to our family home, and back to all the journals and spell books that kept our family, and the town's, history. I needed to find out who Adelaide was, what was going on in the town during that time, and exactly where the wards began and ended during that time period.

"What powers do you have right now? Besides heating water for baths and making a raccoon your familiar?" I noted that demon-heated water didn't seem to ever grow cold. Now that was a trick I could get behind.

"I have my full powers inside this summoning circle. There has been some degradation over the last century, so I believe some of my power may go past the circle's edge."

"But if so, why wouldn't we have sensed it?" I asked. My sisters and I maintained the wards. I was particularly sensitive to any weaknesses or breaks. How the hell could a magical space have existed smack in the middle of our area and us—me—not notice it?

"I don't know, my witch."

I shivered at the "my witch" thing and gripped the edges of the trough, preparing myself to exit the bath.

"Do not try to get out without my assistance," Hadur

warned. Then he spread a fluffy pink towel across the floor, stacking two lime-green ones by the side. I made a mental note about Diebin's interesting choice in colors, then braced myself for the pain of being lifted from the tub.

It wasn't as painful as I'd imagined, probably because Hadur's warm hands on my wet, slick body were sending me back into erotic fantasy land. He held me upright until I got my balance and was able to lean on a nearby chair. Then he picked up the towels and got to work.

Being naked and gently dried off by a gorgeous man ranked up there in my top five life experiences. Top three, actually. No, actually this was my top life experience, although I was hoping that the towel-drying moment would soon be knocked out of the top spot by something more orgasmic. As in an orgasm that wasn't self-induced, or self-induced with the aid of a battery-operated device.

Once I was dry, Hadur carried me to the bed, covered me up with the cozy pelts, then got to work putting clean and dry strips of fabric on my wooden splint. That pretty much ended any sexy-times impulses on my part. By the time he was done, all I wanted to do was lay very still and hope the pain went away. Or at the very least, diminished to a more tolerable level.

"You think Diebin could pick up some more Tylenol next time he makes a Walmart run?" I asked. "Or possibly get behind the pharmacy counter?"

"I will ask him, but communication isn't always clear with Diebin. He often returns with something completely different from what I asked him to bring."

Hence the Tiger Beat magazines, no doubt. "I'll take my chances," I told him, wishing I'd been the sort of woman who'd kept pain relievers in her purse. I really didn't have much of anything in my purse, or much of a purse at all. I tended towards the minimalist when it came to accessories, probably because most of my day was spent in front of a forge. Half the time I left my purse at home and ended up with just my phone and a wallet hastily shoved into the side door pocket of my truck.

"We don't have much in the way of choice for dinner." Hadur headed over to the shelves beside the fireplace. "No animals came into my circle today, so there is no fresh meat. Diebin was supposed to bring some back this morning, but I believe he ate it before he returned."

Damn that raccoon. "So, what did he bring instead?"

"This, and this." Hadur held up a scented candle and a pack of playing cards. "Oh, and this."

Ugh. Another Tiger Beat magazine. "So, what are our dinner choices?"

He set down the candle, cards, and magazine and looked at a line of cans on the shelf. "We have chili, tuna, tomato soup, or something called chicken a la king."

"You're joking." Call me weird, but I had a secret addiction to that horrible, disgusting chicken a la king. "Do you have any more bread from breakfast? Can you make more toast? Because I would kill for some chicken a la king on toast right now."

He gave me the side-eye, then pulled a can off the shelf. "I live to serve, my witch."

"Keep talking like that, and I'll be putting more than chicken a la king in my mouth." I grinned and leaned back against the pillows, the ache in my leg nearly forgotten.

It was oddly domestic, me half-dozing on the bed in the cozy cabin while an incredibly hot guy cooked me dinner. Diebin came back, dragging a plastic shopping bag full of who-knows-what just as Hadur was pouring the chicken a la king over my toast. The raccoon dropped the bag, bounding excitedly over to the plate.

"This is not for you," Hadur scolded in a tone that made

me shiver a bit. "You ate all of our bacon this morning, so you have to eat cat food tonight instead." The demon turned back to the plate, mumbling something about how cat food probably tasted better than this stuff.

He brought the plates over, lit the pumpkin spice candle which still had its clearance sticker on the side, and we ate. Hadur may have preferred cat food, but I thought dinner was amazing and settled back with a contented sigh to watch the demon clean up the dishes and pans. A girl could get used to this. All I needed was a glass of wine. And maybe a not-broken leg.

"Let's see what Diebin brought us tonight," Hadur said, picking up the plastic bag.

I came to attention, crossing my fingers and hoping for bacon. Or Tylenol. Or maybe bacon and Tylenol.

The bag held a travel-sized Yahtzee game, a spatula, the salt half of a blue ceramic salt and pepper shaker, and something from the cosmetics section.

"Nail polish?" Hadur held up the bottle of bright pink polish.

My eyebrows shot up. "How the hell do you know what nail polish is?"

Oh, yeah. That incredibly old Cosmopolitan magazine.

He shrugged. "Diebin brought me an In Style magazine a few months ago. I know all the spring colors and fashion trends and can assure you that Meghan Markle did indeed wear that Dior dress better."

Yikes, the man was more in touch with the feminine than I was. "If you haven't noticed, I'm not really a makeup kinda girl. This shopping trip was a big miss, Diebin. Hope you do better next time."

"When you've been confined to a summoning circle for over two hundred years, no shopping trip is a miss," Hadur announced. "Everything is an opportunity to learn and enjoy, to expand your horizons just a bit."

That had to have been the weirdest speech ever, especially since it came from a war demon. "So, you're going to paint your toenails? Or Diebin's?"

"From what I could glean out of the In Style and GQ magazines, men do not paint their toenails." He waved the bottle. "So, I am going to paint yours. And while they are drying, we will play this game."

I went to protest, only to shut my mouth, forcing a hopefully authentic-looking smile on my lips instead. This guy had saved my life, splinted my broken leg, fed me, helped me pee, got me a hot bath. He was waiting on me hand and foot, pledging to serve me forever—which hopefully included some sexy-times stuff once I wasn't in so much pain. Outside of the broken leg, this was pretty close to a fantasy experience. If the guy wanted to paint my toenails and play Yahtzee, then I wasn't going to say "no."

But first, I had an idea. "Do you think if I wrote a note to my sisters, Diebin could deliver it?"

Hadur frowned in thought. "I doubt he'd know who your sisters were in town, but he could take the note to somebody, leave it on their doorstep, perhaps. Diebin doesn't like approaching strange humans or anyone else. He had a bad experience fifty-three years ago and would not like to risk being shot again."

I winced, wondering if he'd just been nicked by the bullet, or whether his deal with Hadur got him some sort of immortality in the bargain. Clearly though the raccoon was a few hundred years old, he'd been given some life-extending benefits, but I didn't know if that made him bulletproof, or an immortal raccoon, or what.

Either way, this was my best chance at getting rescued. Although at this point, I was less concerned about getting "rescued" and more about making sure my sisters knew where I was and that I was okay. Tearing a page out of the Yahtzee score sheet, I wrote as detailed information as I could about where I'd gone off the road and my current situation, then folded it and handed it to the waiting raccoon.

"Thanks, Diebin. You do this and I promise to cook you up some bacon once I'm back home and my leg is healed."

The raccoon scampered out the doggie door. I set up the Yahtzee, then watched while Hadur painted my toenails. It was surreal, but then again, the last forty-eight hours had been pretty surreal. The storm. My accident. This sexy demon in the woods rescuing my ass, taking care of me, painting my toenails.

I'll admit they looked nice. Not that anyone would ever see them since I spent most of my life in work boots or sneakers. Maybe the cat I planned on adopting from the shelter would appreciate the gussied-up toes in the ten minutes my feet were bare in the shower, but that was probably it.

I glanced at Hadur, who was concentrating as he applied the last bit of polish to my right little toe. What would happen when I set him free? If I *could* set him free. It might take a while for me to find the proper way to do that, but it was the least I could do for the demon who'd saved me. Even if he hadn't saved me, I felt terrible for the guy, trapped here for hundreds of years, his only contact with the outside world whatever Diebin could steal and bring back to him. I know he'd pledged to be mine and serve me, but as erotic as that all sounded, I wasn't sure how it would play out in real life. A demon sex slave sounded good between the covers of a novel, but he wouldn't "owe" me anything for releasing him, and it would be horrible for me to expect indentured servitude or slavery in return. I'd set him free, eventually when I figured out how to do it, and he'd probably just go back to hell.

But I couldn't help fantasize a bit about an arrangement like Cassie had with Lucien. I didn't know Hadur very well, but we seemed to be hitting it off. It would be nice to have someone to come home to besides a cat. It would be nice to have someone to talk to, to spend the evening with, maybe even to work with me. And sex...sex would be really, really nice.

Yep, I had a wild imagination. A forever-after with a demon was a far-fetched fantasy of my repressed romantic side. The realist in me was thinking I might get a roll in the hay before this guy headed back to hell. Honestly, I'd take it. It was better than nothing.

But that romantic side wanted more. Maybe, just maybe, she'd finally get what she wanted.

Hadur sat back and admired his work, then set the nail polish aside and scooted up to the spot on the bed where I'd arranged the Yahtzee game. I explained how things worked, then we got to rolling.

"So, tell me about being a war demon," I said as I added up my four-of-a-kind score.

"It's pretty much like it sounds. When there's a conflict stirring up, I pop out of hell and check it out. Get things moving. Bring stuff to a head. Once I establish momentum, I head back and let everyone take it from there."

I frowned. "I'd envisioned you doing the stirring. And seeing things through to its conclusion. Oh, you should try for a full house on that one. If you don't get it, you'll still have three twos."

He eyed the dice, then took my advice. "There is no need for me to do any stirring. Humans are perfectly capable of working up resentment, unfairness, anger, and envy on their own. The job for me is in making sure that doesn't fester, that they get it out into the open. Sometimes that's through peaceful means, but mostly it's through violence." He rolled the dice. "Yes! You were right. I did get a full house."

I took the dice while he noted down his score. "So, you're like the dude who lances a boil," I teased. "You get the unenviably gross job of making sure the infection gets out and the healing can begin."

"Sadly, no. Rarely is there healing. Always enough of an infection lingers that I find I'm back in a few generations to do it all over again. Sooner, sometimes."

I grimaced, taking a chance score on my unsuccessful large straight attempt as I mulled over his words. "So, you've been stuck here for two hundred years, but there's still been wars and conflicts. I would have thought locking you up would stop all that."

Maybe that's what the summoning witch had been trying to do? Stop wars? Although confining someone, even a demon, for hundreds of years was a pretty shitty way of achieving world peace.

"I'm not the only war demon in hell. Yahtzee! Yes!" He wrote down the score and passed me the dice. "Even if we were all stripped of our powers or locked away, there would still be conflict. Instead of small, easily solved conflict, there would be war on a huge scale—a devastatingly huge scale. Our job is to bring conflict into the open before it grows into something monstrous."

"Like World War Two?" I scowled down at the dice, trying to decide if I should risk my bonus or take a zero on that troubling large straight.

"I read about that in newspapers and books Diebin brought me." Hadur shook his head. "Arestius's work. He's a lousy excuse for a war demon. He never should have let things get that far before stepping in. They should have sent someone else."

"Like you?" I smiled over at him, noting that he seemed to be blushing.

"I do my best," he commented modestly.

"Well, you certainly rock in Yahtzee." I compared our scores. "You should play against Sylvie sometime. She wins everything."

Sylvie had the gift of luck. She helped me out sometimes when I needed a specialized enchantment, but where she really excelled was in luck posies and charms. Sylvie wasn't skilled enough to win the Mega Millions, but she always came out a few bucks ahead on scratch-offs, cleaned up at raffles, and was damn near unbeatable at board games. Clue, Monopoly, Life, you name it.

"You said you have six sisters?" Hadur asked as he put away the Yahtzee game.

"Yep, six." I yawned, snuggling down into my furry blankets. "Cassie is the eldest and the strongest of all of us. She's the one who is shacked up with Lucien. I'm the next eldest. Then there's the twins Sylvie and Ophelia. Then Glenda, who is the only one of us who has any ability in healing, although Ophelia is a paramedic and is skilled in divination. Go figure. Then Adrienne who as I said earlier has this thing going with animals, like some sort of pied piper. Then the youngest is Babylon. Who does *not* do sex magic, in spite of her very unfortunate name."

The demon laughed. "And what does this baby sister of yours do?"

"Necromancy. I know. Weird, huh? We're all pretty weird. Cassie wouldn't even practice magic for years and years— well, except for that time she set her ex-boyfriend's pants on fire. Babylon insists everyone call her Lonnie because she hates her name. Ophelia looks like she's auditioning for a grown-up Wednesday Addams part, or maybe as a back-up for Nine Inch Nails. Adrienne talks to cockroaches in her spare time. Sylvie is a sex therapist specializing in alternative lifestyles or something like that. Glenda is probably the closest to normal of all of us, and she'll talk your ear off about the benefits of seaweed enemas and fish oil smoothies."

"And what about you?" He sat down on the bed beside me.

"Welder. Farrier. Possibly soon-to-be-cat-owner. I enchant things. Metal especially, although I'm really proud of that towel I did for Pete's bar. Fear the towel."

"And?"

I squirmed, not wanting to tell him. We all had our burdens, especially Cassie who'd raised us when Grandma died and Mom took off. My burdens were that I'd heard them—I'd heard the night that Dad left, when Mom was pregnant with Babylon and I was only six years old. I knew that Grandma was afraid—for the town, for us, for herself, that the werewolves would take over if she couldn't keep them in check. I knew why Mom left, and although I hated her for it, I understood.

I was the keeper of the secrets. And I was the one who lived alone, who would probably die alone, carrying those secrets to the grave with me.

Well, alone except for that cat I planned on adopting sometime soon. Maybe when my leg healed.

"Keep your secrets, my witch." Hadur smoothed my hair back, then leaned down and kissed my forehead. "Someday I hope you share your burden and let these things see the light of day before they grow and take root in your soul."

Spoken like a morbid demon. Actually, spoken like a war demon whose job it was to bring conflict to the surface so healing could begin—even if that healing was short lived.

CHAPTER 8

HADUR

*D*iebin came back sometime around midnight, having delivered his note. Whoever had received the missive would find themselves minus three pounds of bacon and a dozen eggs. I gave the raccoon two of the eggs in appreciation, with the promise that I'd share tomorrow's breakfast with him. My witch would have her bacon. And with the note delivered, soon someone would arrive to take her home.

The thought caused me more distress than anything in the last two centuries. Having her here was sweeter than freedom. She made me laugh. I cherished her company. I loved caring for her, providing for her. I wanted her, and from the heated glances she sent my way, from the way her breath hitched and her pulse raced every time I touched her, I knew she wanted me, too. It was torture, but I held myself back, wanting our first time together to be one of unbridled passion, without worry about her broken leg or the bruises she still sported across her chest and legs. Her family would probably be here at daylight, and then she'd be gone. Would she continue to want me once she left?

Would she truly set me free as she promised?

I had mixed emotions about that. The usual arrangement was that a witch would request a task and in return the demon would be granted their freedom, returning to hell after the task was completed. I didn't always relish these tasks, but such was the way things worked between demons and witches.

But this witch was different. I got the idea that my freedom would not be in exchange for any service on my part, that she considered my freedom already earned by my assistance in helping her, or actually just her duty without any need for recompense on my part. I loved that she had such a big heart and a sense of moral duty, but the thought that I would be set free and returned to hell bothered me.

Would I ever see her again? In the course of my infernal duties, could I somehow squeeze in extra time to visit her? That spoiled, pampered Lucien got as many vacations as he wanted, but my requests for them had never been granted. Not even Satan wanted a war demon roaming among the humans with no purpose, potentially causing widespread violence. The only time I was allowed here was as part of my job and if I was summoned.

And if this last summoning was any indication, I wasn't sure I wanted to go through that again. Being called out of hell, only to find myself trapped for two hundred years? If Bronwyn hadn't found me, how much longer would I have remained here?

I looked over at her, feeling a very unfamiliar emotion. Fear. Fear not that she'd leave and forget her promise to free me, but that she'd be unable to do so, that she'd maybe die before breaking the circle that bound me. I'd remain here, possibly forever.

Alone.

Or worse, she'd free me and send me to hell, not caring if

she ever saw me again. It would be that good deed, that nice thing she'd done for the demon she'd found imprisoned in the woods, the one who had helped her from a smashed vehicle and cared for her. I feared that I would be nothing to her, when in such a short time, she'd become everything to me.

It was the fear that made me go to the bed, laying down beside her and gently gathering her into my arms. Her hair was soft and silky, red-brown like the autumn leaves. Her skin warm and soft, shivering under my touch.

I wanted her so badly, but she was hurt and needed sleep. Besides, it wasn't what *I* wanted that mattered, it was what she wanted. But in the meantime, there was no harm in lying next to her, lending her my warmth, thinking of all the other things I'd like to do to her.

Something prickled at the back of my neck, a sense that another had entered my circle. Animals came and went all the time, but in over two hundred years, I'd only felt this feeling twice before—when Bronwyn came crashing through the boundary with her vehicle, and when the werewolf had arrived.

Only a witch could free me from this place. When I'd seen that the trespasser decades ago had been a werewolf, I'd been inclined to ignore him. He was the one who'd attacked me, claiming I was illegally living on their territory. It was a fight to the death—his death. War demons often have that effect on others, increasing their anger and willingness to fight. He hadn't backed down, and I could hardly comply with his demands to leave.

But *this* trespasser…. Diebin had taken Bronwyn's note to someone, and the most likely scenario was that they'd come to rescue her. In the middle of the night. In the dark. I smoothed her hair back, placing a soft kiss on her cheek before sliding out of bed and into my clothing. Diebin stirred by the fireplace, his eyes glowing an eerie shade in the reflected light. I gestured for him to stay, wanting someone here to guard my witch just in case the being outside was more foe than friend. Yes, she was a witch and most likely perfectly capable of defending herself, but she was also injured, and I knew firsthand how fierce an angry raccoon could be.

Moving silently to the door, I listened for a moment, then eased it open just enough to slip out into the night.

A fingernail moon shone faintly behind thin clouds, but I didn't need the light to see. With a quick glance backward at the cheerily lit cabin, I transformed into smoke, rolling along the ground, and approached the intruder.

Not a witch. Not that spoiled arrogant demon she'd said her eldest sister had ensnared either. No, this was another werewolf.

Perhaps things had changed in the last few decades, but I doubted it. As a demon of war, I was skilled at sensing malevolent intent. What had that note of Bronwyn's said? Had the witch-sisters sent this creature thinking my witch was in danger? Was this Lucien's doing? We'd certainly had our disagreements in the past, but I hadn't seen that demon in over two hundred years. Surely, he'd be more concerned about the well-being of a witch, the sister of *his* witch, then any old grudges. And Lucien, as entitled and self-absorbed as he was, wasn't likely to send a werewolf to do his dirty work.

Maybe I was just being paranoid.

Drifting behind a tree, I transformed, deciding my demon form was more likely to send the sort of message I wanted. Then I stepped out from behind the tree and into the view of the werewolf.

The wolf held up his hands. "I mean you no harm. I'm just here for the witch."

My heart sank. This was it. I wasn't sure if I was more

upset that my time with Bronwyn had come to an end, or that her sisters had distrusted me so much they'd sent a werewolf to retrieve her. This must be Lucien's doing. He'd turned them against me. Lucien distrusted me.

But that was my problem, not Bronwyn's. She needed to be home where her healers could help her. She'd promised to release me, and I just needed to be patient and trust that she'd do so. And as for the rest…I'd pledged to be hers, to serve her, but if she didn't want the service of a war demon, then I would just return to hell.

Figures. I finally met a witch to partner with, one I wanted to do more than partner with. I'd finally met a witch I felt I could bond with, one I actually liked, one I enjoyed spending time with, one I wanted to make mine in every sense of the word. Finally, I met a witch I felt I was destined to spend all eternity with, and she might not want me.

"We appreciate your taking care of her," the werewolf told me. "To show our gratitude, we would like to offer you a gift. Are you…are you staying here long?"

"I hope not." I peered at the werewolf, suddenly realizing that he would hardly know my fate. "I've been trapped here for over two hundred years. I cannot leave this area until the witch frees me."

The werewolf shifted his weight. "We never come down this part of the mountain. Two hundred years? No one has known you were here for two hundred years? And you can't leave or anything?"

That warning prickled at the back of my neck once more. What was Lucien planning? Maybe the other demon would make sure Bronwyn never freed me. Maybe Lucien was behind my imprisonment here so long ago and wanted to make sure I stayed here, undetected, trapped forever.

But that didn't matter. What mattered was making sure

my witch was safe and with her people and receiving the care she needed to get better.

"No one beyond you and Bronwyn knows I am here," I replied. "She is sleeping now and it's dark. Did you want to stay and move her in the morning?"

"No, we need her tonight. I can see just fine in the dark and I'm strong enough to carry her."

"You're strong enough to carry her up the side of the mountain alone, in the dark?" Clearly, I'd underestimated these werewolves. Perhaps that one I'd encountered decades ago had been a weakling of their species.

"Yes." The werewolf scowled. "I'm in a bit of a hurry. Her sisters want to see her and make sure she's okay."

Of course they did. I motioned for the werewolf to follow me and led him back to the cabin.

"Stay here," I told the werewolf, remembering how uncomfortable Bronwyn had been about her nudity. She most likely wouldn't be happy to have this werewolf come inside when she was covered only by some pelts. And if she wasn't bothered by the werewolf seeing her naked, then I was.

The werewolf lurked outside the door as I went in. Bronwyn was awake and out of bed, wrapped in a sheet. She was holding onto a small frying pan with one hand, balancing herself against the bedpost with the other. Her reddish-brown hair was a tangled mess. The air sparked with the scent of her magic and sex. Both stirred me. Her magic. Her pheromones. The warmth of her skin, the softness of her hair, how she'd cried out my name when I pleasured her in the bathtub.

I was letting her go. I was letting this witch walk right out of my life, possibly to never return, and it was killing me.

"They're here for you," I told her.

She lowered the frying pan, her brow creasing. "Who? My sisters? Why didn't they come in?"

"They sent a werewolf to retrieve you."

The frying pan came up again. "A werewolf? Why would they send a werewolf?"

"I don't know. They're *your* sisters. He said they're anxious to see you. That's why he's here in the dark of the night. He says that he's strong enough to carry you up the mountain."

Her frown deepened. "Ophelia would have come with him with her medical supplies. Cassie would have come. Actually, they all would have come crashing through the woods. They would have never sent someone else. And especially not a werewolf. This…this isn't right."

I glanced toward the door. "I didn't necessarily get along with Lucien in hell. It could be that he doesn't trust your sisters with me."

She laughed. "Then he would have come himself, not sent some werewolf. Who is it? Which werewolf?"

"I didn't ask his name," I told her, feeling like an idiot admitting that.

Her expression told me she was feeling the same. "You were going to hand me over to some werewolf without even asking his name? Let him in. Hopefully it's Shelby, and you just can't tell male and female werewolves apart. I mean, I have a hard time telling them apart sometimes."

I opened the door and the werewolf entered, eyeing me cautiously, then glancing over to where Diebin sat, cleaning a paw. "You okay?" he finally asked Bronwyn.

"Stanley. Why are you here?"

"I'm here to get you, to bring you back. We got your note. Dallas said to come get you."

"You got my note?" Bronwyn shot a scowl at Diebin, who ignored her.

"He's a raccoon," I explained. "Two-legged is two-legged to him."

She nodded, then turned back to the werewolf. "Do my sisters know I'm here?"

He hesitated. "Dallas sent me. He was going to let your sisters know. I'm supposed to bring you to the compound. I'm guessing we'll either drive you down to the town, or your sisters will come up and get you."

Bronwyn tightened her grip on the frying pan. "No."

The werewolf blinked. "No, what?"

"No, I'm not coming with you. Let my sisters know I'm here and they can come get me in the morning. Until they arrive, I'm staying here. With Hadur."

Stanley threw up his hands. "Come on, Bronwyn. Dallas told me to fetch you. You're gonna get me in trouble."

"Last time I checked, I wasn't Dallas's bitch," she countered. "Now get going. If you're afraid of Dallas, go ask Cassie for asylum, or go over to Clinton's faction and join them. I'm sorry if you're going to get in trouble, but I'm not coming with you."

He eyed me, clearly sizing me up. Then he looked at the frying pan in Bronwyn's hands. "What did you do to the pan?"

She lifted it, spinning it around. "Remember Pete's towel?"

The werewolf flinched. "Sheesh, Bronwyn, why you gotta be like that?"

"Because you're a werewolf, and werewolves have a habit of getting physical. Now get out of here or prepare to face a demon, a raccoon, and a witch with an enchanted frying pan. And if I were you, I'd be most scared of the raccoon."

Stanley glanced over toward Diebin, but it was clear he was more intimidated by the frying pan than any of the other threats facing him. "Fine. But Dallas is going to be pissed."

"Yep, and I'm just terrified of Dallas Dickskin," Bronwyn drawled. "Go. Now."

She waved the pan, an eerie blue light snaking up around the edge. Stanley squawked and ran out the door with inhuman speed. The moment he was gone, the light vanished. Bronwyn lowered the pan and slumped down to the bed, her face pale. I raced to her side, easing her on the bed and gently lifting her leg.

"Thought I was going to pass out or throw up for a moment there," she said, her voice breathy and strained. "Barely got myself upright in time. I didn't want him to know how hurt I was."

"But you know him? It sounded as if you're friendly with him."

Bronwyn gasped as I settled her leg on a few pillows and covered her with the furs. "Stanley's not a bad guy. Got a temper when he's drinking. Likes to brawl, but he's okay."

"But you don't trust him?" Clearly, she didn't if she had refused to go with him.

"I don't trust *Dallas*. Right now, I don't trust any of the werewolves." She took a breath and leaned her head back on the pillow. "When I wrecked, when my truck went down the mountain…I don't think it was an accident. My brakes didn't work. My emergency brake didn't work. I was up at the werewolf compound doing some work for them when the storm was coming in. It would have been the perfect time to screw with my truck. They could have blamed it all on the weather. Even the rockslide could have been their doing. It all would have looked like an accident."

I sat on the bed beside her. "These werewolves want you dead, but you were doing work for them at their place of residence? Why would they want to kill you? And if they wanted to kill you, why are you helping them?"

She scowled at me. "I'm not an idiot. I didn't know they

wanted to kill me when I went up there to do welding for them. I could be wrong. It just seems like a crazy coincidence that my brakes went out in my truck during a storm when I was leaving the compound, and halfway down the mountain, that a rockslide sent me over a cliff into a remote part of the mountain where nobody ever goes."

"But why would they want you dead? Did you screw up the welding job you did for them?"

Bronwyn glared at me. "I don't *screw up*. Not my enchantments and not my welding. As for the werewolves wanting me dead…I don't know. Cassie definitely got on their bad side recently. She's been coming down hard on them, making them alter pack laws so they comply with the laws of Accident. No more exceptions to werewolves. That means she's offered sanctuary to some of them who wanted to leave the pack."

"Sounds like a good reason to kill your sister, but not to kill you," I countered.

"It's not just what Cassie has done, it's what she—what all of us Perkins witches—are going to do. We're in favor of allowing more than one wolf pack, of allowing wolves to choose if they join a pack or not, of limiting the authority of the alphas and making them subject to the laws of Accident. Dallas doesn't want that. Actually, Clinton doesn't want that either, but Dallas especially doesn't want it."

"Again, sounds like a good reason for him to kill Cassie."

"Except I'm the bird in the hand, right there at his compound. Opportunity. And we're close. If I were to die in a horrible tragic accident…well, Cassie wouldn't be as motivated to interfere with werewolf affairs. She'd be devastated. She'd be grieving."

She wouldn't be the only one, I thought.

"Maybe I'm just being paranoid." Bronwyn sighed. "I mean, if Diebin took my note to them, I can see Dallas sending someone to get me and getting the honor of presenting me to Cassie like he was giving her a present or something, thinking we all owed him now for bringing me up the mountain and letting me stay the night in the compound."

"Or he never told your sisters and never intended for you to make it off this mountainside alive," I added. "Would Stanley kill you if this Dallas told him to?"

Bronwyn shivered. "Dallas is the alpha, and Stanley is a wolf who does what he's told. So yes. He wouldn't like it. He'd feel bad about it. He'd make it as quick and painless as he could. But yes, if Dallas told Stanley to murder me, he'd do it."

I reached out to touch her cheek. "I won't let them take you. I promise that I won't let anyone but one of your sisters take you from me."

She smiled. "I appreciate that, but we need to seriously think about defense. Even if we can get Diebin to deliver a message to a non-werewolf next time, we might have to face an attack before my sisters arrive. I don't know if Dallas is going to send a dozen wolves to drag me out of here by force, or try to blow up your cabin, or something."

"Blow up the cabin? They have weapons to do that?"

"Everyone has weapons to do that. It's pretty much household cleaner shit nowadays. But I don't think he'll go that far. Dallas won't want to risk burning down half the forest, or worse, alerting Clinton's faction that there's something going on on this part of the mountain. They've got a bit of an internal issue going on right now, a war of their own. They'll want to do this quiet and stealthy like, and to make my death seem as much like an accident as possible."

"I already told that werewolf that I'd been here for two hundred years, that I couldn't leave this area," I mused. "So even if they don't know you're hurt, they'll know you'll stick close to me, and there's nowhere I can go outside this circle."

"So, we need to be prepared for a dozen wolves in the dark of the night." She stirred as though she was going to get up, then slumped back with a gasp. "Correction, you need to be prepared. I don't think there's much I can do right now to help you."

I was a demon—a war demon. I didn't need a witch's help to fend off even an army of werewolves. I could handle them, not just by fighting them, but by turning them against each other. They had internal strife? A faction that had split and was warring against them?

Good. That was totally my jam, as they said in the Tiger Beat magazines. Let them come. Let them cross into my circle. I'd have them killing each other before they got within a hundred feet of the cabin. I wouldn't even need to lift a finger.

But that wasn't something Bronwyn needed to know. At least not now. She'd been nervous about my being a war demon—scared even. Let her see the dark side of me later, when she might be more willing to accept and even understand it.

"I'll stand guard while you sleep. Diebin will ensure you awaken if you need to defend yourself. And you have the frying pan."

She began to laugh. "Uh, yeah. The frying pan. I lied, Hadur. I couldn't do anything to that pan besides the pretty blue lights. By the time I'd gotten out of the bed and managed to get the sheet around me, I was so exhausted and in pain that I couldn't enchant my way out of a paper bag. The only thing I could have done with that frying pan was whack Stanley over the head with it. And I would have had to hobble my way over to him with a broken leg first."

I scooted the pan over near her hand. "Well, just in case. Here's your weapon."

She wouldn't need it. I'd take care of the army of were-wolves before they were more than ten feet inside my circle. But I knew she'd feel better if she had some weapon at hand.

"Maybe in the morning I can enchant a few things." She ran a finger around the edge of the frying pan. "This. My nippers. If I'm strong enough, then maybe a fork or two."

"I'll give you my power," I promised. "You'll still need to be careful about physical exhaustion, and I can't do much about any pain, but I can help with your magic."

"Thanks." She reached up and ran her fingers through my beard, tugging me closer. "I'm pretty good at enchanting things. Mostly metal objects, but if I'm really motivated, then I can do other things as well."

"Like the towel?"

She blinked. "Towel?"

"You told the werewolf that you'd done the same enchantment on the pan as you had on somebody named Pete's towel. What does the towel do?"

She grinned. "You don't want to know. Just suffice it to say that you should fear the towel."

Fear the towel. This witch was so very strange—and I was absolutely falling in love with her.

CHAPTER 9

I'm not sure how I managed to sleep at all that night. Probably because Hadur stayed in the bed beside me, spooning me and making me feel safer than I'd ever been in my life. Diebin stayed outside, no doubt prowling the perimeter of the circle as a guard. Although I'm pretty sure Hadur would have been instantly awake and ready if someone so much as stepped a toe over the magical boundary of what had become his home.

Something about his nearness—Hadur's, not Diebin's— made me stronger, refreshed. It had only been four days since my accident and I had no right to feel as good as I did. Even my leg felt better. Yes, it still gave me sharp twinges of pain, a reminder every time I tried to do something beyond my injured abilities. Yes, I was hobbling around the cabin on uncomfortable, uneven, makeshift crutches, dragging a splinted leg behind me. But I knew that broken bones shouldn't feel quite this sound four days in. I didn't even have any Tylenol for Pete's sake, and I was hopping around like a champ.

The moment I stirred, Hadur kissed my forehead and got

up to fix breakfast, apologizing that it would be oatmeal as he'd instructed Diebin to stand guard and not go on a thieving expedition to Walmart. I was more interested in raiding the demon's very strange collection of clothing that had been acquired by the raccoon over many decades.

"Do you…do you actually wear this?" I asked, holding up a bright purple paisley rayon shirt with the biggest pointed collar I'd ever seen. I looked at the tag, and realized that there was no way Hadur could ever wear this shirt. It was a men's medium. He'd never get this thing buttoned across his massive chest.

Mmmm. His massive chest. It was so perfect. Just thinking about it made me want to drag him back to bed. Why hadn't he made any more moves on me since that day with the bath? I mean, the guy seemed to have a perpetual hard-on around me and clearly welcomed every caress and touch of mine, but that was it.

Crap, was I going to have to make the first move here? It wouldn't be easy with a broken leg, but I'd do it if that's what it took to get me some action here. A girl could only take so much sexual frustration before she exploded.

"I have not worn that shirt, but I kept it in the thought that I might be able to use it for some purpose eventually."

"Well, it's polyester, so you can't start a fire with it or anything." I put the shirt on, easily buttoning it down the front. It fit across my chest and midsection with ease. I was stupidly tall for a woman—just a hair over six feet—so the sides barely skimmed my hips and the front came right to my crotch. My ass was still hanging out from behind.

It was silky. And the purple paisley cracked me up. Plus, with the top buttons undone, it looked rather sexy, like I was wearing my boyfriend's shirt from 1970. "What do you think?" I asked.

He didn't even look. "I like you better naked."

"Yes, I know that, but I can't exactly fight werewolves naked. And if my sisters eventually figure out that I'm missing and show up, I might not want to greet them naked with a splint on my leg."

He glanced over. "It's lovely. Especially because your ass is still visible under the hem."

Yes, that was a problem. It meant I'd be especially motivated to make sure I was facing anyone—werewolf or witch. Or if I really got pissed, I'd turn around and moon them. I can't think of anything that would send a bunch of attacking werewolves fleeing more than the sight of my naked ass. Except maybe my naked boobs and snatch.

"I wish I had some sweatpants that would go over this splint," I complained. "Or shorts. Or even underwear. Not the thong kind, though. That would sort of defeat the purpose here."

"I like you naked," he repeated.

I rolled my eyes. "We've been over this. It's not like you're walking around in the buff."

Hadur looked down at his jeans and t-shirt. I wondered how many pairs Diebin had hauled to the cabin before the raccoon had managed to get the right size?

"Do you want me to walk around naked?"

Yes. Yes, I did.

"This human form has rather sensitive skin," he continued. "I'd end up scratched, bruised, and bleeding every time I went outside the cabin."

"That's my point exactly," I told him. "Fighting werewolves naked with exposed sensitive skin isn't wise. And we're not running a nudist camp here. I don't want my sisters showing up with us both in the buff. Or Lucien. Crap, Cassie will probably bring Lucien along as well. That guy goes everywhere with her."

Hadur growled. It was a sexy sound, although I don't

think he intended it to be. "I don't want Lucien seeing you naked."

I turned around. "Then you best help me do something about my bare ass."

It turned out the best solution was to tie a shirt around my waist. I still had to be careful not to flash anyone, but it would do.

Besides, I'd gotten rather fond of the 1970s paisley shirt.

After our oatmeal breakfast, I assembled the items I wanted to enchant on my bed, made myself comfy, and pondered what I wanted to do. Magical Taser? Confusion? Fear? Temporary blindness?

Blinding someone with a fork would be hysterical.

The big challenge with all these was that most of my enchanted objects required contact for the spell to take effect. I wasn't sure I wanted to be close enough to a were-wolf to stab him with a fork for him to be temporarily blind. What I really needed was to enchant these items with a magical word to activate the spell. Abracadabra or something. Basically, I needed to create a wand.

And I wasn't sure I had the skill to do that, even with Hadur lending me his power.

"I'll need some paper and a pen," I told the demon. "And a knife or something to etch the spell onto the metal."

He brought the items over to me, then hovered, watching as I scribbled a few runes on the paper. No, that wouldn't work. Electrifying the nippers would mean I'd get shocked as well. Which wouldn't be pleasant. I crossed out the runes. Hadur lurked over my shoulder.

"Can you go somewhere else?" I scowled up at him.

"I thought you'd want my energy to help with the spell."

He pouted. The demon, a war demon of all things, was pouting.

"I do, but I won't be ready to cast the spell for a while. I'm not fast. I can't do these things on the fly. I might not be able to do them all under this moon and astrological conditions, but I'm going to try. Either way, it's going to take me hours of prep at a minimum before I'm ready to charge anything. So, go...chop a tree, or grab a rabbit for dinner, or read Tiger Beat or something because I can't work with you watching me like this."

He grumbled something and headed off. By the time he'd returned and started dinner, I'd made some progress. At this rate I'd possibly have one enchanted weapon by nightfall. Hopefully the werewolves would hold off for a few days so I could do the frying pan and a fork as well, otherwise it was going to have to be me and my stun-gun nippers to the rescue.

The smell of roasted meat was starting to permeate the cabin. My stomach growled, but I pushed on, almost done with the inscribing part of the spell. After dinner we'd charge it. I hated to do these things on an empty stomach.

Hadur stiffened, dropping his spoon onto the table and pivoting toward the door.

Shit. It wasn't even dark yet. I hadn't even had time to charge the spell on the nippers. Damn it all, I felt so helpless here in bed with a broken leg and nothing but a frying pan to defend myself with.

"Someone crossed into the circle?" I asked. I wondered if I was strong enough to do a quick enchantment on the frying pan. I doubted I could bluff my way out of this one as I'd done with Stanley. How many had Dallas sent for me? Would my sisters ever find my body? Or the smashed truck? And what would happen to Hadur? He'd remain trapped here and now that the werewolves knew where he was and his situation, they'd ensure no one stumbled upon his cabin ever again.

He came to stand protectively in front of my bed. "A

group. I can't tell how many. Maybe six, maybe ten. I don't think it's more than twelve."

I gently eased my splinted leg to the floor and stood, holding onto the bedpost and checking to ensure my paisley shirt and butt-wrap covered all the important parts. "You go intercept them. Diebin and I will take care of whoever makes it past you to the cabin."

Suddenly I wished Diebin had stolen a shotgun and some shells from Walmart. A fry pan wasn't exactly a distance weapon, and I wasn't in any shape to be grappling hand-to-hand with any foe, let alone a werewolf. Hopefully Hadur was badass enough to take on half a dozen of Dallas' finest. If not, I wasn't going to let them kill me, not without giving a few of them some serious concussions with my frying pan.

Hadur went to the door only to have it fly open, smacking him in the face. There was a flash of light that made me gasp and cover my eyes, and a voice shouted a spell of protection.

I nearly cried, because I recognized that voice.

"I'm okay, I'm okay!" I called out. "Stand down. I'm okay, and with friends."

I blinked open my eyes and saw them—all six of them. My sisters were piling into the cabin, knocking aside chairs and the table in an effort to all squeeze into the room. Hadur was pinned half behind the door, looking bewildered. Diebin had run and hid in a corner. I didn't blame him. My sisters had that effect on people.

Everyone erupted into conversation at once. Ophelia sat a black bag on the bed and immediately started checking me over. Glenda poured something from a thermos and shoved it into my hands.

"What the fresh hell is that shirt you're wearing?" Sylvie asked. "It looks like you stole it off a bad '70s porn actor."

"Are your toenails painted?" Babylon pointed at my feet. "Nail polish? When did you get all girly on us, Wynnie?"

I held up my hand, the one not holding a cup of whatever it was that Glenda was urging me to drink, and asked everyone to please settle down.

"I'm okay," I repeated once they were all silent. "Besides a broken leg, that is. My truck went off the side of the mountain. Hadur found me and brought me back here and took care of me."

Everyone turned to look at the demon who stared back. "It's like a coven crammed into my cabin," he commented. "A loud and intimidating coven."

"Thank you for helping my sister." Cassie approached him. "Thank you so much for taking care of Bronwyn. When I think that she could have died in that crash, or lay there in that truck for days waiting for us to find her…"

"Yes, days." I snapped. "Four days. Did no one notice I was gone for four damned days? What the hell?"

Everyone looked down at their feet.

"I'm so sorry, Wynnie," Cassie finally said. "I left a few messages on your phone, but sometimes you just don't call back right away. It wasn't urgent. I figured you'd call when you got a chance. You're kinda…you're kind of a loner. I don't want to constantly be all up in your business."

She was right. If it wasn't urgent, sometimes it did take me a while to return a call. And I did occasionally go a week without talking to my sisters, even Cassie. "Well, you're forgiven. Maybe I need to start wearing one of those emergency alert necklaces or something."

"A GPS tracker," Adrienne suggested. "Some people put them on their dogs."

Great. Bronwyn and the pet Beagle, both with tracking collars. I felt so loved.

"How did you all finally find me?" I asked them. "Did the werewolves send you a message? Did someone see my smashed truck from the road?"

Cassie's eyebrows went up. "Well, let's see...you didn't show up for family dinner tonight and weren't answering your phone. None of us had heard from you in a few days, so we got worried. Ophelia did a divination that showed you were hurt and trapped somewhere, so we got *really* worried. She and I managed to do a tracking spell with Lucien's help, and it brought us here." She turned to smile at Hadur. "Sorry for the entrance. We weren't sure what was going on or what we were going to find in here."

"Is Lucien with you?" I seldom saw Cassie without the demon any more.

"No, Ophelia got something in her divination that led her to believe him coming along would be a bad idea, so I had to convince him to stay behind with Aaron."

"I'll bet that went well," I drawled.

"Let's just say that there's probably going to be a lot of sex on the agenda tonight."

"So why is this Hadur living in the middle of the woods— on the side of a mountain owned by the werewolf pack inside the town wards?" Glenda asked.

"With a raccoon!" Adrienne squealed, kneeling down to better see Diebin. "Oh, look at you, you cutie, you! I know you! You're the little guy who was stealing Joe Swanson's chickens, aren't you? Come here so I can give you a hug."

Diebin hesitated, then dashed forward into Adrienne's arms. She stood, cuddling the raccoon, who seemed absolutely enchanted by her. That's the way it always was with Adrienne. And this was far more adorable than her cuddling spiders or slugs.

"Hadur is a demon," I told my sisters. "Someone summoned him two hundred years ago and never showed up to complete the deal. He's been trapped here in a summoning circle since then."

"And he made a deal with our new friend here to bring

him food and supplies from outside the circle." Adrienne added, scratching Diebin behind the ears. "Smart boy. Very smart boy."

I wasn't sure if she meant Hadur or Diebin.

"A demon." Cassie took a step back from Hadur. "What sort of demon?"

"War," he replied. "I know your bonded demon, Lucien. And no, we do not get along. I'm sure that's why your sister's spell advised he not come."

"But you can't leave the cabin?" Cassie asked.

"I can leave the cabin, but not the confines of the summoning circle."

"It's just under an acre," I told her.

She frowned. "That's big. I mean, I don't know much of anything about summoning demons, but from what I do know, the circles tend to be no bigger than a twelve-foot diameter, not nearly an acre in size."

"So…what does that mean?" I asked.

Cassie shook her head. "I'm not sure. Maybe the summoner meant for him to be here long term, or possibly forever? That's why the size is bigger than normal?"

"Right," I scoffed. "How nice of her. 'I'm going to confine a demon for all of eternity in a remote area of a mountain, but I'm a nice witch so I'll make sure he has a bit of room to stretch his legs.'"

"Can we discuss this later?" Ophelia asked. "Maybe after we get you somewhere we can X-ray that leg and get a cast on it?"

"I can't just walk out of here, in case you didn't notice," I told her. "I'm assuming you guys hiked in. And I'm also assuming nobody mastered teleportation spells in the last four days."

Ophelia scowled. "Shit."

Everyone turned to look at Cassie. We always turned to

look at Cassie. She'd taken care of us when Mom hit the road. She was the one who hosted Sunday family dinners. She was the strongest among us, the one who now "ran" the town in spite of our elected mayor and sheriff.

"I can't teleport, even with Lucien's help," Cassie said. "Maybe a helicopter?"

"And where would someone land a helicopter?" Sylvie spoke up. She'd been mostly silent until now, checking out the books over in the corner and also checking out Hadur.

"People do rescues for climbers and boaters with helicopters and those basket things that they lower down," Babylon chimed in. "Who do we call for that? If we had a cell signal here, I'd Google it."

"There's a state emergency helicopter for transporting critical accident victims," Ophelia said. "Maybe they have a basket thingie?"

"But it's not really an emergency," I added. "How much are they going to charge for that? Guys, I don't think my insurance is going to cover airlifting me off the side of a mountain, and in case you didn't notice, welders and farriers don't make the big bucks."

"We'll chip in for it," Cassie replied. "Ophelia's right. We need to get you somewhere to get checked out, X-rayed, and a cast on that leg. We can't carry you up the side of the mountain, and we're certainly not getting a truck down here and back up again. Hell, we barely made it down here. Sylvie bitched the whole time about snagging her pants on briars and rocks."

"That was you bitching about your pants, Cassie," Sylvie shot back. "It's my shoes I was worried about, not my pants."

"Maybe I should just stay here." I glanced over at Hadur who was wisely staying out of the way and remaining silent. "Ophelia can get a portable X-ray machine and cast my leg here."

"And leave you here in the middle of nowhere for the six weeks it takes for your leg to heal?" Ophelia argued.

They all shot quick surreptitious looks at Hadur. I knew what those looks meant. My sisters didn't like the idea of leaving me alone with him for weeks. A demon. A warmonger. I was hardly the weak flower of the family. I welded. I forged horseshoes. I didn't give a damn about snagging my pants on thorns or breaking a heel in the woods. But I was their sister, and right now I had a broken leg. That made me someone to be pampered and fussed over, someone who they weren't going to leave for weeks with a war demon in the middle of nowhere.

Hadur held up his hands. "I will do everything in my power to keep Bronwyn safe and help her recover, but I agree that she should be in a place with skilled healers. And I fear that she may not be safe here."

"What? Why?" Cassie exclaimed, turning to me.

It all seemed so silly in the light of day, but Cassie did need to know, just in case there was an issue with the werewolves—with Dallas.

"I was working on a welding job up at the pack compound, and that storm was coming in. I left right when it hit, and going down the mountain, my brakes suddenly failed. Nothing. Flat to the floor nothing. No parking brake either. I was trying to steer the truck in the pouring rain and hopefully do a controlled crash when a rockslide knocked my truck off the road and I went over the cliff." I shuddered at the memory.

"And you think the werewolves did something to your truck?" There was that look in Cassie's eye—that look she got when she was two seconds from setting an ex-boyfriend's pants on fire.

"I take good care of my truck," I told her. "I mean, maybe it was an accident, but maybe it wasn't. Then Hadur had

Diebin take a note I'd written to someone, and he evidently took it to the werewolf compound. Last night Stanley shows up, insisting that I'm supposed to let him carry me out of here and to the compound in the middle of the night. He said Dallas sent him, that Dallas had sent a message to you. It just felt…weird. I was scared and suddenly with the accident and all I got paranoid. I told him I wouldn't leave unless you all came to get me yourself."

Just saying it made me feel like a complete idiot. What if the brake failure had truly been a mechanical issue? What if Dallas's motives had been reasonably benign? What if I was freaking out over nothing?

"Now I'm even more positive that you're not going to remain here," Cassie insisted. "Dallas has been pissed at me since the thing with Shelby. I can totally see him doing something like this to break our focus and resolve."

"I'm calling for a helicopter," Ophelia said, getting out her phone.

How mortifying to be air lifted out in a basket. I'll admit when I'd told Hadur I wanted my sisters to come and rescue me so I could get home and get real medical attention, I hadn't thought about the logistics. And I hadn't thought about leaving him here, all alone, possibly with a bunch of werewolves who might want revenge for his protecting me from Stanley's attempt to haul me off the other night.

"First, you're not calling for anything here because there's no cell service, remember?" I told her. "Secondly, I'm not leaving. Ophelia, you can X-ray my leg with a portable device and bring stuff to cast it here, can't you? I'm fine otherwise. I'll heal in…" I looked at Ophelia.

"Twelve to fourteen weeks. Or sixteen depending on the break."

Ugh. That was a long time—a really long time.

"Four if you drink the smoothies," Glenda countered,

waving a hand at me to get going and drink the one still in my hand. I took a sip, nearly gagging at the taste. Maybe twelve weeks would be preferable to this disgusting stuff.

"I'm not leaving you here," Cassie snapped. "You need medical attention. You need to be home where we can help you, where you're not in the middle of nowhere. You need to be where I'm not worried about werewolves attacking you in the middle of the night."

I eased down onto the bed, trying to decide how I was going to get my splinted leg back on the mattress while I was still holding a frying pan and a smoothie. Mattress. Huh. How had Hadur managed that one? I couldn't see Diebin dragging a mattress through the woods from some store. Was this one of those straw-stuffed pioneer mattresses, because it didn't feel any different from my mattress at home. If it was, though, where had he gotten the straw?

None of these were questions I needed immediate answers to, so I put them aside, slugged down the horrible smoothie, handed Glenda the empty glass, and gently eased my leg back onto the bed. "Not leaving. Figure it out, girls, because I'm not leaving."

"Is she always like this?" Hadur asked.

"Yep," Cassie told him. "Always."

"Fine." Ophelia put her phone away. "I'll come back with equipment and something to cast your leg. And crutches."

"And my smoothies," Glenda added. "And some healthy meals because I don't think you've been eating right."

"And reading material." Sylvie held up one of the Fifty Shades books. "I've got a whole library of kink. And some vanilla stuff too, just in case rope play isn't on the menu with a broken leg."

"Diebin knows where we all live and how to reach us if you need to send a message," Adrienne chimed in, kissing the raccoon on the top of his head. "He knows us all by name, so just tell him who the message should go to."

"Yeah. And if you need me to raise the dead, then just call me." Babylon drawled. "No? No one wants me to raise the dead? Figures."

"I'm not leaving you," Cassie insisted. Again, the message was that she wasn't leaving me with Hadur, in the middle of nowhere, hurt, with possibly a werewolf attack in the future.

I rolled my eyes. "I'll be fine. As soon as Ophelia is done with me and I manage to choke down a couple of Glenda's smoothies, I should be feeling okay enough to defend myself. Heck, I was almost ready to enchant this pair of nippers when you all got here. And Hadur isn't going to let anyone hurt me. He's a demon. He's a freaking war demon. Some pansy-ass werewolves aren't going to get past him."

"I'm not leaving you." Cassie walked over and sat down on the edge of the bed. "Ophelia can bring back some clothes for the both of us. I'll sleep here with you. He can sleep somewhere else. Like outside the cabin somewhere else." She glared at Hadur.

Seriously? I wasn't like this when she had started banging Lucien. My sister, the hypocrite. "You have a job—a lawyer job. You can't stay here with me for twelve to fourteen or sixteen weeks—"

"Four," Glenda announced.

"Four weeks," I corrected. "You have a job. And I'll be fine."

She bit her lip. "I'll work from here."

"With no cell service and no electricity. What are you going to do, file briefs via smoke signal? Or send Diebin in with a packet of handwritten notes every day?"

"Mack and Russ will cover for me. The law firm partners are sphinx. They'll understand. I'll…I'll take a leave."

"We'll take turns," Babylon told her. "If each of us stays for a week, rotates staying here with Bronwyn, then you won't have to deal with those sphinx assholes you work for."

Cassie glowered down at the floor, her jaw set in that typical concrete firmness that told me she didn't like our youngest sister's suggestion one bit. As much as Cassie had chafed at having to raise the lot of us when she was only thirteen, she wasn't one to give up her authority easily. She'd bitch and moan about it, but she liked being in charge. She liked taking care of us all. And she honestly didn't trust anyone else to do as good a job as she did. It was like we were all little children still in her mind. Which was funny since I was only two years younger than her.

I reached out a hand to grip her shoulder. "Tonight only, Cassie. Then let someone else take a turn babysitting your thirty-one-year-old sister if you're that worried. You can come out when you get off work to check on me if you need to, just to make sure we haven't all been slaughtered in our sleep by werewolves."

"Not helping," she muttered.

"I'll be fine. Hadur and I will be fine. And by tomorrow morning, you'll realize that and stop thinking I need to have my whole family standing guard outside a cabin."

"You've got a broken leg, Wynnie." She reached out a hand to touch my cheek and I saw how worried she really was. "You're hurt. I don't know this demon. And if the werewolves really did cause your accident…"

"I don't know that. I'm just conjecturing, and maybe I'm a little overly paranoid because the werewolves are jerks and in the middle of a turf war. As for Hadur, I trust him. And my leg…well it will heal in twelve or fourteen or sixteen weeks."

"Four," Glenda reminded me.

"Four," I corrected myself. "Ophelia and whoever else wants to help carry shit down a mountainside and through the woods can come back with medical stuff and clothing.

Oh, and books. I need the books from the attic. I need all the diaries from two hundred years ago and any spell books that might have information on demons and demon summoning."

If I was going to be stuck here for four weeks in a cabin with my sister with no electricity, running water, or Wi-Fi, then I might as well get some research done. Besides, I was determined that by the time I walked out of this place, Hadur was walking out of here with me. Whether he chose to stay or go at that point was his decision, but I wasn't going to have him trapped here for a moment longer than necessary.

"And smoothies and sexy reading material...." Sylvie was writing it all down on a paper towel with a pen she'd managed to find somewhere.

"And a porta-potty," I added. "One of those portable ones. Chocolate. Wine."

"We're gonna need more than one trip." Ophelia rolled her eyes.

"We've got it," Sylvie said. "I'll help Ophelia carry it all. And if we can't get it all in one trip, I'll come back later with more."

My sisters all moved toward the door—well, all of them aside from Cassie.

"I'm staying here. Tell Lucien..." she appeared a bit flustered about what they should tell Lucien, and I knew why. The demon was going to bust a gasket over this whole thing. He barely let Cassie out of his sight. He'd even taken to lurking around the courthouse during her trials, and although she'd threatened to set his extremities on fire, I could tell she kind of liked the stalkerish behavior. Weirdo. Her, I mean, although he was plenty weird as well.

"I'll tell him you and Bronwyn are having a threesome here with another demon." Sylvie grinned. "I'll even go into details."

"No, you will not!" Cassie shouted at her back. "Sylvie! I mean it. Do not tell him that!"

She turned to me with a groan once they'd all left. "I'm so dead. So. Dead."

"Lucien is a selfish, arrogant asshole, but I can't see him killing the witch he bonded with," Hadur commented. "You can make his life miserable, you know."

"Oh, she already does that," I told the demon. "On a regular basis. They're quite a good match, you know."

"I'm regretting my decision to stay here already," Cassie told me. "And we didn't even get to eat dinner. Please tell me there's something to eat in this place."

"I think Hadur has a rabbit on the fire, although it's probably a bit past well done at this point." I motioned over to the shelf of cans. "Or you can take your pick. I think there's some tuna over there if Diebin didn't already have it for dinner."

"I had a pork loin in the oven," Cassie muttered as she inspected the canned goods. "Pork loin. Fried apples. Roasted brussels sprouts."

"Did I mention that I just drank Glenda's fish-oil and barf smoothie? So don't be complaining about burnt rabbit and canned tuna."

"Your sister puts barf in her potions?" Hadur looked horrified.

"No, she doesn't," Cassie assured him.

"Yes, she does," I countered. "Barf. Poop. Pureed slugs. Eye of newt."

"She does not." Cassie glared at me then took down the can of tuna. "It's not even packed in water. Oil. Who eats tuna packed in oil?"

"Raccoons evidently," I told her. "Beggars can't be choosers."

She ate the tuna while Hadur and I had ultra-well-done rabbit. Then while Hadur and I played a rousing game of go-fish, she roamed the cabin, picking up various objects until she had an entire handful of random household utensils, candles, and scraps of paper and napkins.

"What is she doing?" Hadur hissed.

I shrugged. "Spells. You're going to see how incredibly paranoid my sister can be when it comes to protecting her family. Got any twos?"

"Go fish. She's doing spells with spoons?"

"Yep."

"Are there any light bulbs?" Cassie called out.

"Oh, yes, for all those lamps that we can't use because Hadur doesn't have any electricity. Got any sixes?"

"Hey, it's my turn. Got any fours?"

"How about batteries? Oh, can I use this flashlight? And this packet of mouse traps?"

"Take whatever you want," Hadur told her.

I handed him my fours. "You might not want to tell her that. She'll strip the cabin. You'll find all your belongings strewn along a perimeter enchanted with magical spells."

"I thought you did the enchantments of the family?" he asked me, putting down his set of fours.

"I do. And I do them better than Cassie." I glanced over at her, noticing that she didn't refute my statement. "She's the only generalist of the family, which basically makes her a jack of all trades."

"And master of none," she added wryly.

Cassie was master of plenty. She was the most powerful of any of us. And where I could out spell her when it came to enchanting metal, she was just as good at enchanting other objects. Well, she would have been just as good if she'd practiced her magic over the last few decades. Right now, she had some catching up to do.

"Need me to help with any of that?" I asked.

Cassie looked at her armful of objects. "How's your pain level? Can you manage some of these spoons?"

The pain in my leg was now more of a dull ache. Actually, the dull ache wasn't as bad as it had been this morning. And it had improved quite a bit after I managed to choke down Glenda's disgusting smoothie.

"I can do the spoons right after I finish with the nippers I was working on," I told her with far more confidence that I would have had just a few hours ago.

I moved the cards aside, aborting the go-fish game that Hadur had been on the verge of winning anyway. She set the spoons down beside me next to the nippers, the frying pan, and the fork.

"What are you planning for all these things?" I asked.

"The mouse traps will be alarms. The flashlights are temporary blindness. These?" She shrugged. "I was thinking something defensive."

"Wouldn't knives be better for that?" Hadur asked.

"Probably if we were looking to stab someone." I picked up one of the spoons. "Stabbing a werewolf isn't really that effective. They heal fast. It just pisses them off unless you can somehow launch two dozen knives into them at once."

"And spoons work better?" Hadur was clearly perplexed.

Actually, I was too. Normally I had all sorts of brilliant clever ideas for things to enchant, but I was tired, and despite my confidence just a few minutes ago, I was worried I wouldn't have the strength to do more than the nippers and one of the spoons—whatever I intended on doing with them.

Spoons. "I think I'll do a sap energy spell," I said. "Were-wolves are absolute babies about that sort of thing."

"Sure you don't want to do a towel spell?" Cassie asked.

I didn't have the strength to do one towel spell, let alone half a dozen. That thing was complex. Doing the one for Pete had taken me weeks, and I didn't have weeks here.

"No, I'll do the sap energy." I ran my fingers around the spoon, thinking of the incantation, the focus area, the sigil I'd need to trace, and the energy I'd need to somehow pull together.

"Can I help?" Hadur asked.

"That pen knife over on the table? I need to scratch sigils in each spoon just like I did with the nippers, only different sigils."

He shook his head but got up to retrieve the item. "I meant can I help as in can I contribute to the spell?"

Cassie sucked in a breath. "No, you cannot."

I bit back a smile, knowing what she was thinking. When Lucien granted Cassie his energy for a spell, it was downright erotic.

"Yes, he can. I was going to have him help me with the nippers as it was. If you want me to enchant all these spoons, then I'm going to need help. He can help."

She glared at me, then at Hadur. "Go outside while I speak with my sister."

He scowled back. "It's my home. No, I'm not going outside."

I rolled my eyes. "Please step outside. Cassie's going to give me a sex ed talk and she doesn't want to do it in front of you."

There was a bit of a staring match between the two, then Hadur headed outside with an exasperated huff.

"Has he...have you..." Cassie made a rude gesture with her hands.

"We've gotten to second base. Or maybe third base. I didn't really memorize what happened at which base, so I'm not really sure. Let's just say up until this morning I've been naked, and there was some fun involving a bathtub."

My sister clapped her hands over her ears, then paced a

few steps before lowering her hands. "He's hot, if you're into that muscled, mountain man look—"

"I totally am," I interrupted her.

"He's a war demon." Cassie glared at me. "And you're not…you're not all that experienced with guys, Bronwyn. I don't want you to get hurt. I don't trust him, and I don't want to see you fall for some good-looking, studly, jerk of a demon who will break your heart."

"Like Marcus did to you?" I totally threw her ex-boyfriend, the 'ho of a panther shifter, in her face. "Look, I get that you're protective. You've always been that way to me, to all of us. And it's kind of a sisterly obligation to warn us that we're about to make a terrible mistake in the boyfriend department. Warning taken. But I'm a grown woman, Cass. I'm thirty-one damned years old. And just because I haven't had a manly shaft breach the walls of my virtue doesn't mean I'm a fool about men. Have some faith in my ability to make a decision, please."

She smiled, and her eyes glistened with something that might have been tears. "Okay. But if he turns out to be an asshole, if I find you crying out by the pond over him, then shit's gonna get real."

"Pants-on-fire real?" I teased.

"Oh, way more than pants-on-fire real," she shot back. "No one hurts my sisters and gets away with it."

And now my eyes were glistening with something that might have been tears. "I love you, Cass."

She plopped down beside me on the bed, knocking spoons and the frying pan aside to put her arm around me. "I love you too, Wynnie."

We hugged for a moment. When we separated, I dried my eyes on what I hoped wasn't the werewolf pelt. "Good. Now that we're in agreement on all that, let's get to enchanting some objects."

CHAPTER 10

BRONWYN

*W*e both got to work inscribing runes on the odd assortment of objects. It went much faster with Cassie here than it had this morning. She instinctively knew the right order, the correct symbols, the added embellishments that would make the magic more precise. Hadur returned, making us tea and watching us work. When it came time for me to enchant my nippers and the spoons, he crossed over to my side.

"I'm not watching," Cassie proclaimed, although she didn't seem prudish enough to actually leave the cabin. Or even avert her gaze. Hmm. Maybe she was going to watch after all.

I didn't care. I'd seen Lucien help her with magic before and while the energy exchanged sort of brought the emotional and physical nature of their relationship into clear view, it wasn't as if they were naked and doing it on the kitchen table or something.

"State the purpose of the magic, my witch." Hadur's voice was deep and rumbling and I shivered, wishing my sister would have gone to take a walk or something.

"When the witch who holds the nipper-wand says the activation word, it will shoot a non-lethal shock of electricity into the being it's pointed at," I told him. "The handle is shielded so the spellcaster doesn't get zapped. It's a varying electrical shock, so if I point it at a werewolf, the nipper-wand sends a bigger shock than if I point it at a human."

I was a bit proud of that. Many hours this afternoon had been spent in figuring out the correct rune combination to make sure if I accidently shot one at an innocent bystander in a fight, I wouldn't fry them. It was a pretty cool magical weapon, in my opinion. And they would still function as my favorite pair of nippers. Trimming hooves and zapping werewolves all in one handy-dandy tool. What more could a girl want?

Hadur nodded. "Seems straightforward. I'm ready when you are, my witch."

I shot a mischievous glance at Cassie. "Then put your strong, virile hands on my nippers, you sexy hunk of demon, you," I told Hadur in a breathy voice.

Cassie made gagging noises in the background. The war demon smirked, then took hold of the nipper-wand, his hands overlapping mine.

I began to chant, the magic leaping to my skin, swirling around me with increasing speed. Hadur's deep voice joined in, and I gasped as his magic flooded me. Everything tingled, warmth settling down low in my core. Wow. I might not be the most experienced woman in the world, but this felt totally erotic.

I closed my eyes, falling into the feel of his magic as I mixed in my own and chanted the energy into the nipper-wand. Once it had been charged, I changed my words, sealing and holding the magic to the object, and ended the spell.

Instantly I felt the loss of his magic. I still tingled with magical aftershocks of the experience, awash in happy satisfaction, but I definitely wanted more. More of his magic, more of him.

I'd not even known this demon a week and I was falling in love with him. It wasn't just the sexual attraction, or the magical attraction, it was him. I couldn't imagine not having him near me. I wanted to wake up with him in my bed, to share meals with him, to play Yahtzee in the evenings, to just *be* together.

In the back of my mind was the worry that things might not work out, that once I freed him he'd return to hell, or that he'd get bored with me and one day he'd be gone. But I couldn't worry about that. All I could do at the moment was think about the now, and how this felt so right, how it felt like the beginning of something amazing.

We went on to charge the spoons, which had a far simpler and less sexy magic attached to them. And when we were done, I felt oddly invigorated. Normally this much magic would have completely exhausted me and sent me to my bed for a good eight hours, but I felt ready to do more—well, not much more, but I probably could have managed another spoon or two. And if those werewolves stormed into the cabin tonight, I would be ready with spoons and a nipper-wand.

"Well, at least I know what Lucien and I look like when we're doing it," Cassie drawled. "I feel like I need a shower, now."

"Thought you weren't going to look," I reminded her.

"Kinda hard not to look with you two moaning and gasping like a budget porno over there," she teased.

I brandished a spoon at her but couldn't help smiling.

"My turn." Cassie turned to face her objects and began with the flashlight, wiping a bead of sweat off her forehead when she'd finished. "Whew. This is harder than I remember.

I'm so used to having Lucien help me that I forgot the toll this sort of magic takes."

Cassie was a powerful witch, the only one of us who could perform magic on the fly, but enchanting objects wasn't her strength like it was mine. She could do it, and with practice probably do it better than I could, but it still took more effort.

"Do you want me to finish?" I pointed to the other objects.

"No, I've got it." She motioned toward my leg. "I don't want you to overexert yourself. Drink more of Glenda's smoothie and relax."

I grimaced at the half-empty glass by my side, the second one I'd had so far. It was soooo bad. How could Glenda make the most amazing meals, each one a culinary delight, but her potions always taste like a dirty gym sock?

Cassie finished her magical work and I finished the smoothie. We were discussing whether or not to open the bottle of wine when Hadur abruptly stood.

"There is a demon at the edge of my circle."

For a second I panicked, thinking that the werewolves had managed to add a demon to their attacking army, then I relaxed and laughed.

"Cassie, your stalker has arrived."

She shook her head, but there was a hint of a smile curling one corner of her lips. "I'm going to kill Sylvie. She probably told him that threesome story like she threatened."

Maybe. Maybe not. Lucien wouldn't have liked the idea of Cassie spending a night away from him, let alone a night in a cabin with another man…demon. I looked at the door expectantly, but no demon flung it open.

Hadur chuckled. "He can't enter the circle. No demons can cross while the boundary is in place. You might want to go to him before he gets too upset and starts burning down the forest."

"Shit!" Cassie leapt to her feet and ran out the door. "I'm coming!" she shouted. "Don't start breaking or burning stuff, I'm coming!"

"That's what she said," I joked, easing off the bed and reaching for the crutches Hadur had made for me. There's no way I was going to miss this.

Hadur helped me hobble through the dark of the forest, at one point picking me up and carrying me. The whole way I could hear Cassie and Lucien arguing—hell, I think the whole mountain could hear them arguing.

"You're not staying here," Lucien snarled. "I don't trust those werewolves not to try something. I can't get through this barrier to help you if you need me. Who's in there? What demon is in there? Your sister said a war demon, but I can't tell through this darned barrier."

He didn't say darned. In fact, he said an entire string of descriptive vulgarities that was too much for even me to repeat.

"I'm the demon in this summoning circle," Hadur announced as we walked into the moonlit clearing and gently set me on my feet…foot.

There was a sudden heaviness in the air. Both demons squared off like gunfighters about to go at it.

"You're not staying in there with *him*," Lucien snarled. "And neither is your sister. Both of you get out of that circle right now. Get over here by my side. Right now."

Bossy stalker. Times like this I wondered what my sister saw in this guy. Then Cassie let loose a diatribe peppered by a whole lot of f-bombs, fire sparking at the end of her fingertips and I realized she was more than capable of putting this demon in his place.

Lucien backtracked. "He's a war demon, pookie. He could

set you and your sister against each other. He could…he could make you lose your temper. You're already having to attend those anger management meetings each week. As much as I love your short fuse, I really don't want you under the influence of a war demon."

Pookie? *Pookie?*

"I'm not influencing her," Hadur snapped. "Or Bronwyn. Give me some credit for having control over my powers, you spoiled, lazy, arrogant hellspawn."

Fire erupted around Lucien's arms. "What did you call me? You might want to rethink your words. I do outrank you, war scum."

"Yes, you outrank me. Nepotism at its finest. What are you going to do, go crying to your father? Whine that a war demon insulted you?"

I put a hand on Hadur's bicep, taking a brief second to admire the muscle under my fingers. "Stop. You just said you have control, but here you are stirring him up. Let's not have a war between the two of you right now."

Hadur growled, my words not registering at all with him. His eyes glowed gold. The bicep under my hand bunched.

I did something I never thought I'd do—I pulled out the woman card.

"Oh, my leg!" I leaned against Hadur, my voice breathy. "I think hobbling through the woods strained…something."

Hadur instantly snapped out of it, his eyes turning to me in concern. "Should I carry you back to the cabin? Should your sister go get the other sister that heals? Do you need more of that foul-smelling smoothie? My witch, tell me what you need."

I swatted him on the arm. "I need you to stop baiting Lucien. He's my sister's main squeeze, and if things work out between us, you two are going to have to get along. Especially because you'll be sitting across from him every Sunday night at family dinner."

Both demons looked horrified at the idea. Cassie laughed.

"Lucien, relax babe. Let me spend one night here making sure my sister is safe, then I'll be back in your arms. One night. I know you're worried about me, but this is important. My family is important. They'll always be a priority to me."

He did relax. And smile. "Your family, the town. It's all a priority to you."

"You're a priority to me too," she said softly, reaching through the magical barrier to take his hand. "I'll show you how much of a priority tomorrow night. I promise."

Ewww.

"Okay, show's over," I told Hadur. "Carry me back to the cabin, James. Let Cassie and Lucien do some kissy-face in private."

When my sister returned to the cabin, she was glowing with that sappy smile on her face that I was beginning to know so well. And this time when I felt happy for her, I didn't have that usual stab of envy.

CHAPTER 11

BRONWYN

*O*phelia and Sylvie arrived the next morning, loaded down with supplies. Hadur promptly vanished outside with some mumbled excuse about checking the woods for werewolves. I knew that he was really fleeing the overwhelming chaos of having four witches in one tiny cabin.

Three of which I sincerely hoped would be gone by lunchtime. Or dinnertime at the very latest.

But for now, I had some clothing besides my 1970s paisley shirt and makeshift wrap skirt—mostly dresses that didn't require too much work to put on over a splinted leg and a few pairs of sweat pants and t-shirts. There was now a portable toilet, a camp stove, several solar chargers, and bags and bags of chocolate, two bottles of wine, and a disgusting two gallons of Glenda's smoothies.

The battery-operated X-ray machine was courtesy of a veterinarian two towns over who used it for cattle and horses. It made sense. Running half a mile of electrical cord from a field wouldn't have been practical and some barns didn't have a readily available source of electricity. Either way, it limited the sort of X-rays my sister could take—which made her very grumpy.

"Yep. Broken tibia," Ophelia announced, looking at the X-ray on her cell phone. There was no sheet of film with this cool techie device, just a piece of glass that got hooked up via USB. I glanced over my sister's shoulder and looked at the picture. "Although I'm not a doctor, and I'm strongly suggesting you get airlifted out of here and seen by someone who *is* a doctor. But from what I can tell, it's non-displaced and should heal well without surgery."

"Guess I should be grateful," I told her.

She put her arm around my shoulder. "Yes, you should be grateful. When we came down the mountain yesterday and saw your truck…well, I feared the worst." Her voice choked with emotion.

"The only thing that kept her from panic was that the driver's side door was ripped off the hinges," Sylvie chimed in. "We looked inside and saw the blood and the twisted dash, but no dead body. It looked like someone had ripped everything apart with one of those jaws of life things, so we figured someone had gotten to you."

"I assumed it was the werewolf pack, but Ophelia's divination said you were in the woods," Cassie told me. "I'll admit I was a little scared that meant you were lying somewhere, hurt. Ophelia insisted her divination said you were injured, but alive. We just didn't know how injured you were."

I smiled over at her. "Just a broken leg."

I'll admit Cassie's presence was starting to grate on my nerves. She hadn't been here twenty-four hours and I was already giving her less than subtle hints that she should go home. Normally I got along with my elder sister. We shared a bedroom growing up, and out of the whole bunch, she was the one I could normally take on a long-term basis, but the close confines of this cabin and her mother-hen protectiveness and paranoia were more than I could handle.

Yes, they'd been terrified, afraid they'd lost me. I understood how horrible that must have been. It made me realize that if the werewolves were trying to shake up Cassie, to reduce the power of the Perkins witches over the town and the residents, then killing one of us would do the job. Cassie was a neurotic wreck over my broken leg. If I'd been killed, she would have retreated completely, left the town and the werewolves to their own self-government, left everything to fall apart.

We needed to be careful. And we needed to find out what happened to my truck, and the who and why behind the sabotage—if it were in fact a sabotage.

"Yes, just a broken leg." Ophelia squeezed my shoulder then started to pull some gauze and supplies from her bag. "Now I'm going to make you a real cast. It's not gonna be fun. I've got to extend it to cover your leg above the knee and below the ankle."

I grimaced, realizing that this was going to hinder my mobility even more than Hadur's splint. But I did want my leg to be properly stabilized so it could heal correctly. And I could put up with it for twelve to fourteen weeks. Four if I could manage to choke down Glenda's smoothies.

Ophelia unpacked more supplies from her bag and got to work gently wrapping a liner around my leg. She then wet the fiberglass cast material and wrapped it around the liner.

By the time she was done, I had a bright pink cast extending from above my knee to below my ankle. It was heavier than Hadur's splint had been, but it did a much better job of holding my lower leg immobile. No more aches. No more pain every time I moved. And the best thing of all? It was some special waterproof cast that meant I didn't have to bathe in the tub with my leg stuck over the side.

Once it was dry and hardened, I slid out of the bed and stood, taking the crutches Ophelia handed me. I made my way across the room, put the crutches in one hand, and lowered myself into a chair.

"Thank you," I sighed. As nice as it had been to have Hadur carry me here and there, this gave me a level of freedom I hadn't had for days. I could freely move about the cabin without pain, get myself a drink or a book, or even go to the bathroom without assistance. And with those horrible smoothies Glenda had sent, I should be back to normal in a month.

Ophelia held up her hands. "My work here is done. I'll be back to check on you this weekend. If you need anything in the meantime, send me a message via raccoon."

My sisters had discovered the no-cell-signal dead spot encompassed far more than just the area around Hadur's cabin. Pretty much this entire side of the mountain had spotty, if nonexistent, coverage. Cassie would have needed to climb up past the road and up almost to the werewolf compound to get a signal.

And that wasn't something we wanted to do.

Ophelia had carried in the medical supplies, the clothing, and the portable potty, but Sylvie had the heavier load. She was the one with the books. And the wine. And a bag with who-knows-what in it.

"Here are the journals." She set a stack next to me on the table. "From the time period you specified, there were six journals. I also have a copy of the genealogy chart of the Perkins family from that time period. Then I grabbed four spell books that I thought might have information on summoning and releasing demons." She shrugged. "If there's nothing in there, then we'll have to start reading through the other books. I'm not too optimistic on any of this, Wynnie. From what I know, we Perkins witches have never been involved with demons. Well, beyond Cassie shacking up with one, that is."

"What's in the bag?" I asked, dreading the answer.

Sylvie winked and set the bag on the table. "Oh, just a few things for you and Hadur."

"Not while I'm staying here," Cassie protested.

"Yes, well, you'll be leaving before nightfall," I countered with the argument I'd been making since I woke up this morning next to my sister and not the hunky demon.

Sylvie and Ophelia said their goodbyes, both kissing me on my cheek and telling me they'd check in every few days. Six sisters. That was going to be a whole lot of checking in. I fully expected that even Babylon would make a special trip back to Accident just to make sure I was okay, and she generally only came home for Sunday family dinner.

After they left, I turned to my elder sister. "You know, we really need to address the eight-hundred-pound werewolf in the room."

"Dallas isn't that fat," she joked. Actually, Dallas wasn't fat at all. Very few of the werewolves carried any extra weight. There was a lot of social pressure in the pack to look like you spent most of your day at the gym or running through the woods on four legs.

"I mean it, Cassie. They know we're here. Hadur said they avoid this area, probably not wanting to become another pelt on the bed, so they know he's here. Dallas sent Stanley down to get me, so they know I'm here. They're werewolves. They've got an insane sense of smell and they're territorial. They knew the moment you all drove up here yesterday to look for me. They know you're staying here in the cabin. They probably knew the moment Sylvie and Ophelia left."

"Good. Maybe they'll know not to mess with you again." Cassie folded her arms across her chest, a stubborn set to her jaw. "Two witches and a demon? And Lucien pacing my floor back home eager to beat the crap out of anyone? They won't dare mess with us."

Maybe. Maybe not. An entire pack of werewolves—well, a pack minus the dozen or so that Clinton had in his splinter pack—wasn't an easy win even with two witches and possibly two demons. They had numbers on their side and even with demon assistance, we could only do so much. If they hit us hard and fast, there was a good chance we'd be dead before Lucien or our sisters could reach us.

Grief over my death would have shattered the family emotionally. Grief plus the loss of Cassie, the strongest witch the town had seen since Temperance Perkins, would mean the werewolves or other supernaturals who wanted to run things their way in Accident would be unchecked.

"Cassie, we're more vulnerable with you here then with you in the town," I told her. "Go up to the compound. Tell Dallas about the brakes on my truck being messed with. Put him on notice that I'm here and that any attempt to harm me or 'rescue' me will be considered an act of war. Tell him any move against me and Hadur will not only result in the entire supernatural community of Accident including six witches coming down on him, it will result in the entire pack's expulsion from the protections of the town. No more mountain. No more pack. They'd need to try to live under the radar among the humans with the constant threat that they'd be hunted down and executed."

Cassie shook her head. "He'll deny they had anything to do with your truck. He'll be offended I'd even suggest such a thing, insist with wide-eyes that he sent Stanley to rescue you from the big bad demon. Then he'll pinch my ass and try to grope my boobs."

She was right. But I was right, too.

"Of course he'll deny it, but he'll know that you know."

"And I'll know that he knows that I know."

"And he'll know that," I pointed out with a grin. "Put him on notice. Then go back to Lucien before he wears out your floors worrying about you. You guys can check on me every day or so, but you can't stay here. You're driving me nuts. You're driving Hadur nuts. And my best bet for safety is not your presence, but the fear of a harsh reprisal if anything happens to me."

She sighed. "Fine. Honestly, I need to get out of here anyway. I've got cases at work. And Lucien. And I really don't want to see you and that demon using whatever sex toys Sylvie brought in that bag."

"Go talk to Dallas, then come back and let me know what happened. Then go home."

She nodded and stood. "Okay. You get your way. I'm not happy about leaving you here alone, and I'm definitely not happy about leaving you here with that demon, but you're a grown woman. And what you said does make sense."

"I'm the smartest one of the family," I told her. "So go. Do as I say."

She grinned. "Fine. And you might be smart about this stuff, but not about romance. I'm worried about you, Wynnie. Be careful. That demon is dangerous, and for all your sass and swagger, you're too sweet and trusting. Don't let good sex make you ignore all the red flags. Guard your heart. I don't know that I trust that demon out there. Be careful."

She might not trust that demon, but I did. "I'll be careful," I assured her, knowing full well that I'd already made my decision about Hadur.

I dove right into the genealogy and the diaries as soon as Cassie left, only glancing up when Hadur returned to the cabin.

"I thought maybe my sisters had scared you back to hell," I teased him.

DEBRA DUNBAR

"Trust me, if I could have run away, I probably would have." He came over to the table, then stopped to survey Ophelia's handiwork on my leg.

"I can get in and out of bed on my own and hobble around the cabin," I told him. "Although I still might insist that you carry me from time to time, just for the romance of it all."

"I live to serve, my witch."

The words still sent a thrill through me, even though they'd changed. Hadur had originally delivered the statement in a voice of desperation with a vow of servitude. Now they seemed teasing, sexy, less about him being my obedient demon and more about him being my partner.

I liked that. I wanted that. Although the other thing still made for some fun sexy-times fantasies.

"It's very pink." He knelt down to touch the cast.

"I know. Ophelia's quite the comedienne sometimes. Wanna sign it?" I grabbed a Sharpie off the table and handed it to him. "You write your name, or some funny saying, or draw a picture. It's traditional when someone has a cast."

He uncapped the marker and drew a sigil. Then, with a grin, he encircled it with a heart.

"Is that you?" I asked.

"That's me. We're normally very cautious about others knowing our sigil, but since I'm currently trapped in a summoning circle, it really doesn't matter."

"So, if someone used this sigil to summon you, they'd get nothing because you're already trapped?"

"Yes, aside from a few special circumstances."

"What is used to summon, might be used to banish," I mused.

"Yes, but hopefully you're not going to banish me; you're going to set me free." He handed the marker back to me. "Banishing returns me to hell, and I won't be able to come

122

back unless I'm summoned again, or receive a task requiring my work here, or if I'm granted leave time and given a coin so Charon could transport me here."

"It's a worst-case scenario idea," I assured him. "If I can't free you from the circle, maybe I can banish you, then just summon you again."

He reached out and placed a hand on my thigh, above the cast. "Summoning is no easy magic, Bronwyn. You've told me that you and your sisters do not practice the art, so there is no one to mentor you, no one to assist you in the ritual. There is a good chance if you banish me, that you will try unsuccessfully for decades to summon me back."

"I know." My chest hurt at the thought. "But if I can't manage to free you, then at least by banishing, you would no longer be trapped here. Surely being returned to hell is a better life than being stuck on less than an acre of woods."

"No, because then I would not be with you." His hand caressed my leg, his thumb making little circles on my inner thigh. "Trapped here, I will hopefully still be able to see you, to have you with me. I would rather remain here then be free in hell without you."

Could I do that? Live here with him on the side of a mountain within werewolf territory? With no electricity, no cell service, no place to park a car or truck. Each morning I'd need to hike up the side of a mountain and drive into town, pick up my truck and trailer, and work, only to do it all again the next day. Maybe if I reduced my hours to accommodate the commute. Maybe if we came to some sort of agreement with the werewolves where I didn't feel like I was one full moon away from attack. Maybe we could make this work until I managed to find a way to free Hadur.

I wondered if Diebin would get along with a cat.

"Then it's a plan," I told him. "I'll figure out a way to free you, and in the meantime, I'll stay here off and on. Or maybe move in full time if things work out between us. I need you to be honest, though. If you decide this relationship isn't working, and you want to call it quits, I don't want you to think you need to keep going through the motions because otherwise you'll be stuck here alone. If I can't free you and you want to call it quits, then I'll figure out a way to banish you back to hell. I'll always help you, even if we don't work out romantically."

"You, my witch, are very silly. I'm an old demon. I know my mind. I want you. I want to partner with you, to bond with you, to be with you for all eternity. And your pledge to selflessly assist me makes me want you even more."

My breath caught as he moved his hand higher. "We might want to delay the displays of mutual affection for later. Like, when I'm sure Cassie isn't going to burst through the door later. So hold that thought. I'm going to do some research and try to keep my mind away from what you could be doing with your fingers and other body parts."

He bent down, scooting my dress up practically to my hips. Then he placed a lingering kiss on my inner thigh and stood.

Ugh. I was so not going to be concentrating on anything but the feel of his lips on my leg, the brush of his beard against my thigh. And that was a problem, because these diaries with their outdated language and swoopy cursive handwriting required a lot of concentration.

"These are the diaries and spell books?" Hadur looked at the books, then picked up the bag Sylvie had left. Before I had a chance to stop him, he'd upended it, spilling the contents across the table.

Oh my. Sylvie...well, my sister had outdone herself this time.

Hadur stared at the items. "Your sisters are very strange."

"Tell me about it."

"What is this for?"

I turned bright red. "It's…uh, it's nipple clamps. And don't ask me how I know that. Trust me, it's not from personal experience."

He pulled off his shirt and affixed them to each nipple while I stared with a mixture of admiration and horror.

"Ow. These things hurt," he complained.

"They hurt worse when you take them off," I told him, wincing as he yanked one from his nipple.

The demon sucked in a breath. "Does Lucien know about these? I think they need them in the punishment sections of hell."

"I'm pretty sure Sylvie gave Cassie and Lucien a set as some sort of 'you've got a boyfriend' gift."

He reached over and picked something else up from the table, the one nipple clamp still attached, the other dangling from the chain. "And this?"

I winced. "Anal plug."

"Are you sure your sister isn't a demon?"

"There are days when I ponder that very question."

And there we were, me sitting in a chair with my dress hiked up to just shy of my coochie, Hadur standing over me wearing one nipple clamp and holding a turquoise anal plug when Cassie burst through the door.

We all froze. My sister slapped a hand over her eyes.

"I did not just see that. Nope. Did not see that."

I wrestled my dress back down while Hadur removed the nipple clamp and put them and the anal plug back in the bag.

"All clear," I announced.

Cassie peeked between her fingers, then let out a relieved sigh. "Okay. I talked to Dallas—actually I threatened Dallas. I did a lot of yelling while he acted as though he had no idea what I was talking about. So, he knows that we know, and he also knows that I'm going to bring all of hell down on his furry ass if he so much as looks at you funny."

Maybe not all of hell, but two demons. And witches. And whatever residents of Accident were fed up with the werewolves.

"Good. Now get out of here so we can get back to anal plugs and nipple clamps," I told her.

Cassie backed away. "Leaving! Leaving now! As long as you're sure you'll be okay, that is. There's a flare gun over by the portable potty. Send up a signal if you need us."

And by the time they got here, we'd have either taken care of the situation ourselves, or we'd be dead.

"We're fine," I told her, with more hope than assurance in my voice. "We're fine. Go. Stop worrying."

"Okay, okay. And if you get attacked by werewolves, go after them with the nipple clamps and the anal plug. That's bound to scare them all away."

The funny thing was, she was probably right.

CHAPTER 12

HADUR

I lurked while Bronwyn read, trying to find something to do that wouldn't distract her. Although I really wanted to distract her.

Those sisters of hers had nearly sent me over the edge. Maybe it was because I was a war demon. Maybe it was because I'd spent over two hundred years completely alone in the forest. Either way, all the chaos, the noise, the witch-energy circling around the cabin…it set my hair on edge, made me want to burn down the mountain or explode something.

Or make them all fight.

There were some unresolved issues between these witches, and as a war demon I hated unresolved issues. Air out the grievances, get physical if necessary (and it was always necessary when it came to humans), then hopefully resume with a cleaner, healthier relationship. But it wasn't my place to do that. Well, it was my place, but I hadn't been officially assigned this task, and while I'd never been averse to a little side job in the past, these were Bronwyn's siblings. A small nudge was the most I'd do. For now, anyway.

Even she had secrets that would fester if they remained buried. Her eldest sister had anger and resentment, although of all seven, she seemed the most open about letting her feelings have a voice. Or a fist. That was probably somewhat due to Lucien's influence. I didn't like the demon, but I'd be willing to admit he had his skills—and he was clearly dedicated to his witch.

The others…they had their own burdens, which would lighten considerably if only they shared them. But again—it wasn't my place to interfere in Bronwyn's family. Well, beyond a nudge.

Thankfully Bronwyn managed get the eldest sister to leave my house. Lucien knew he wasn't welcome, but after his one visit, I knew he'd decide protocol be damned when it came to being with his witch. If Cassie stayed, Lucien would be back, prowling around the perimeter of my circle, camping out if necessary. And if the sisters set my hair on edge, Lucien made me want to do more than burn down the mountain.

But they were gone, and finally there was peace in my home once more. Just me and Bronwyn. Now, if only I could keep my hands off her while she read.

"This is interesting." She looked up from the book she was reading and pointed to the genealogy chart. "There are no journals from Adelaide Perkins, but there is one from her elder sister, Celesta. I'm guessing Adelaide was probably between sixteen and twenty from your description of her. She was twenty-six when she passed away."

"That might have been why she didn't return," I said, although when I thought about it, six to ten years was plenty of time to research a spell, or at the very least come back and tell me she was working on it.

"I think she didn't come back because she was afraid." Bronwyn looked up at me. "According to Celesta, Adelaide was very weak for a witch. That might have been sibling rivalry talking, but I really do think Adelaide wasn't a significant force in the Perkins family during that time. Her Aunt Matilda was head witch and running the town, and there was an Aunt Larkspur who was a very powerful second. Adelaide and Celesta's mother, Serenity, was a very weak third."

"How many cousins were there?" I leaned over the chart, looking at the tiny handwriting on the section she was pointing to.

"A lot. Matilda had four sons at the time of the journal I'm reading, and Larkspur had a daughter and two sons." She shook her head. "Male offspring of witches are unusual, so that's really odd. Male witches don't have magic. There are some very rare exceptions to that, but even those witches aren't as powerful as those born female."

"So, the line would have gone from Matilda to her sister's daughters—either Larkspur's, or Celesta, or Adelaide."

"Cousin Marina wasn't well. I'm thinking she might have had the same illness that eventually killed Adelaide because according to the chart, she died a year before her cousin."

"Leaving Celesta to carry on the family name," I said.

"Yes, which is one of the reasons I have her diaries." She held up the book. "We try to keep everything now, but some witches didn't keep journals, just spell books. In the past, a lot of journals were lost or destroyed, but there was always special care taken with the records of those who eventually took over as head witch of the town."

"So, did Celesta say anything in her diary about summoning a demon?" I asked. "The magical energy of the summoning circle was the same as Adelaide's, so it must have been a relative. Plus, I'm assuming your ancestors are the only witches in the area?"

"There's no rule that says we have to be the only witches in Accident," she told me. "In fact, Temperance put up the wards in hopes of this being a safe haven primarily for witches. Few escaped the burning times, so Accident instead became a sanctuary for any supernatural being who wanted to live free. We've just never had other witches come. There aren't many left in the world."

So, it probably was one of her family that had summoned me. "Do you think it might have been Celesta?"

"She's got nothing in her journal so far to indicate that her magical studies might have been going in that direction. I'm not sure if she would have come right out and admitted it, though."

"Because there's something shameful about summoning demons?" I scowled at the thought.

"No, because you're a *war* demon. Which meant whoever summoned you had some sort of violent conflict in mind. We've never been a family of witches that deals with demons, so if one of my ancestors went to the enormous effort to find out how to summon you, then they would have had a particular purpose in mind—something very specific they wanted you to do."

"So, you're reading the diaries to find motive?" I guessed. "To see if someone wanted a person or a group of people to either go to war or to find death at another's hand?"

I doubted they were wanting me to bring buried conflict to a head, like a demon family counselor. No, Bronwyn was right. When witches summoned a war demon, it was usually because they had death in mind.

"Yes, and so far, all I'm finding is a bunch of family intrigue." She pulled a napkin over, uncapped the marker, and began to write. "Matilda was making noise about a second marriage after her husband's death, and Larkspur was worried that union might yield a daughter and ruin her and her daughter's chances to be head witch. Marina and Celesta hated each other. Plus, there was some serious discussion about whether to oust the fairies or not. Pretty much like the discussion over whether to oust the were-wolves or not today."

"So, Larkspur, Marina, and Celesta all had motive." I counted off on my fingers. "And Matilda, if she wanted demon back-up in getting rid of the fairies."

"Adelaide had a boyfriend that dumped her," Bronwyn added. "She might have done a revenge summoning."

"But your family talents don't involve summoning. That seems like a whole lot of work to go to just to get back at a boyfriend."

"Speaking as a man who probably has never been dumped," she commented wryly. "Hell hath no fury like a woman scorned, my friend."

"Understood. But looking back, I don't think Adelaide summoned me. Yes, she was right there by the circle, but she seemed a bit alarmed to see me. And she never returned."

"Maybe she was alarmed because the ritual actually worked," Bronwyn countered. "Adelaide wasn't a powerful witch. She could have been doing the magical equivalent of a Hail Mary and been astounded when you actually showed up. Then faced with you, she might have decided she didn't hate her ex-boyfriend all that much and changed her mind."

"And didn't bother to send me back to hell?" I asked.

Bronwyn shrugged. "Maybe she couldn't figure that ritual out. Maybe she tried and never got it to work. Like I said, she wasn't all that powerful."

"Okay, we'll add Adelaide to the list, but I still don't think it was her."

"If I was a betting woman, my money would be on Matil-da." Bronwyn picked up a book bound in red leather. "Which is my next read. If I can find out who summoned you, then I don't have to look through hundreds of spell books to find the ritual and the research notes. But honestly, these journals are annoying the crap out of me, so if I can't find out by the time I read Matilda's, then I'm diving into the spell books."

I held out a hand. "Let me help. I'll take one, you take the other. Then we can both read spell books."

She hesitated. "These are the journals of my witch ancestors. I don't think non-family should be reading them. I mean, you might find out that incredibly secret apple jelly recipe, or that my great-great-great grandmother cheated on her husband with a satyr."

"Give me that." I snatched the book from her hands and got to work.

Three hours later, I wished I could go back in time and drag this Matilda down to hell. I'm pretty sure she was there already. I'd need to ask Lucien to check for her and maybe give her a little extra punishment because she certainly deserved it. The woman was horribly cruel to her sons. I was pretty sure she'd killed her husband. And I had a suspicion that she'd been involved in the illness that had eventually taken Marina's life.

Her daughter's death had driven Larkspur into a deep depression. She'd withdrawn from town affairs. She refused to do all but the most basic magic. From Matilda's gleeful entries, her sister had become practically a hermit—and no threat at all to her rule. Matilda didn't see Adelaide as a threat and was only slightly wary about Celesta. Her youngest sister barely registered on her radar. Her final diaries were mainly about her ongoing issues with the fairies and her determination to have a daughter and her suspicions that she'd been somehow cursed. Three husbands after her first and she still only had the four sons. From the vaguely worded entries, I realized pregnancy wasn't an issue. She most likely was doing away with any child that wasn't the gender she wanted.

I summarized what I'd read to Bronwyn, telling her that I

thought Matilda might have been the summoner. She certainly had the power. But if I was here to smash any attempt by her sister or her niece to take over, then why hadn't I been released? If I was meant to handle the issue with the fairies, why continue to struggle and not use me? Why just leave me here?

"Nope." Bronwyn held a leather-bound book aloft. "It was Celesta. She doesn't come right out and say it, but I'm pretty sure she was the one who summoned you."

"To take out Matilda? Then why not release me and give me my task?" I asked.

"For one, because Adelaide saw you. Celesta adored her younger sister. I think Adelaide told her about the demon in the woods, and Celesta felt ashamed, like summoning a demon to murder her aunt was something that would tarnish her in Adelaide's eyes forever. I'm really reading between the lines here, but I think she told Adelaide she'd take care of the situation. That's why Adelaide never came back or worked to free you. In her mind, she'd done what she promised—she went to her more powerful older sister and Celesta promised to handle it."

"Then what? She couldn't figure out how to banish me and just left me here?"

Bronwyn paged through the book. "I think originally she meant to keep you as a sort of contingency plan in case Matilda went after her. I mean, Marina was dead. Larkspur was consumed by grief. Year after year, Matilda wasn't having any daughters. Celesta always downplayed her abilities and power, but judging from her diary, she never really felt safe."

I looked down at the genealogy chart. "She lived and ran Accident for thirty years after Matilda's death. That's thirty years she could have freed me or returned me to hell. Instead she died, and any knowledge of my existence here died with her."

"Except for the werewolves, who obviously didn't realize what you were or the circumstances of your entrapment here," Bronwyn commented.

"Did Celesta just forget about me?" I'll admit I snarled a bit with those words. I was bitter. I had good reason to be bitter.

"I think she might have. We're not skilled in demonology. Maybe she thought you just went back after a certain amount of time. Maybe she couldn't figure out how to return you." Bronwyn looked up at me, her eyes soft and full of sympathy. "Maybe she did forget about you."

I swallowed hard and turned away. Was that how it would be with us? Would Bronwyn leave once her leg healed and never return? Would her promises to free me fade in her memory as time went on and she found herself unable to find the correct ritual?

Would I ever see her again?

A hand touched my arm. I hadn't even heard her get up or heard the noise of her crutches on the floor.

"I won't forget about you, Hadur. I won't fail you, and I won't forget about you. Ever."

I turned to face her, pulling her gently into my arms. "But what if you can't find the ritual to release me, Bronwyn? What if I'm trapped here forever?"

She put her hand on my cheek, sliding her fingers down to tangle in my beard. "Then I'll be trapped here with you. Forever. Until my dying day."

That…that would be the one thing that would truly make me feel free while trapped in this summoning circle.

"I'm yours, my witch," I whispered to her.

"And I'm yours, my demon," she replied.

CHAPTER 13

BRONWYN

I was ready to toss these spell books through the window. Except the cabin only had one tiny window. I wondered why that was? If Diebin had been able to lug a feed tub for baths and a giant cast-iron soup pot through the woods, then certainly he could have dragged three or four nice sets of energy-efficient windows.

I'd been through two of the spell books and found nothing to do with demons. Nothing. Clearly there had been some unspoken family taboo about summoning and using demons because not only had Celesta never referred to her actions in her journals, but neither she nor Matilda had anything about hell's minions in their spell books. Had there been a separate book she'd used for this ritual? For the research she'd put into this? Something she kept hidden so others might not see? I was beginning to believe that. If so, I was worried the book might not have survived two hundred years.

One thing I was positive of—there was a book. No witch did this stuff from memory. All the details, all the research, and the initial efforts were meticulously recorded. I had a spell book. Cassie had a spell book. Every one of my sisters had a spell book. To not keep track of these things in detail was the sort of sloppy magical practice none of us would have been guilty of. I refused to believe Celesta was any different. She'd been very exact in the spell book I'd spent the afternoon reading. There had to be another more secret one somewhere.

But where?

I clenched my jaw at the thought that I might not find it, that it might have inadvertently been destroyed. Our family tried to keep all the spell books—not just those of the head witches. Journals we might be more careless of, but not spell books. Even the most powerless of witches might have knowledge we'd need some day. Throughout the centuries we might have changed, our focus shifted, but no one ever took the value of a spell book lightly.

For example, if our house burned to the ground, these things would still be there among the ashes, unharmed. That's how seriously we took our preservation efforts.

It had to be somewhere. And if it wasn't…well, then, I'd need to search the globe for any of the other witches who'd survived the burning times. I'd find the correct ritual. I'd free Hadur.

And if I couldn't, then I'd remain with him until my dying breath. I'd made that promise and I meant it. But I wasn't about to see Hadur trapped, knowing that he'd still be stuck here after my death. No, finding that ritual would be my life's focus.

Sorry centaurs, those blingy horseshoes would need to wait a bit.

"Need a break?" Hadur asked. "I can cook something up for dinner. One of these canned things, or that box of macaroni your sister brought."

"I need to get out of this cabin," I told him. "I'm going a bit stir crazy, and these spell books aren't helping."

He eyed my leg. "With your crutches? We're in the woods. The ground is uneven and it's rocky. Maybe we could just go outside and sit. Get some fresh air. Or I can carry you if there's a certain place you want to see."

I loved that he had this need to take care of me. No one besides Cassie had ever been that way toward me. Maybe my grandmother when I was little. Maybe my mother when I was an infant. But by the time I was eight, both of them had been occupied with more serious matters. And by the time I was eleven, Grandmother was dead and Mom was gone and there was only Cassie.

Two years older than me. She'd done everything she could to mother us, but I'd grown up with her as a peer, sharing a bedroom, hiding under the covers with flashlights, reading at night. Her efforts to make me feel safe were admirable, but I'd seen through them to the scared teenager who was struggling to care for six sisters all while grieving for a beloved grandmother and hiding her fury toward a mother who'd left us all behind.

Mom had her reasons. But her leaving had meant there were few people who'd ever protected me, who'd ever fussed over me, who'd ever put me first.

So, I loved Hadur for his suggestion. And I also knew I couldn't let him coddle me.

"I've got another idea. Let's head out to my truck. I haven't seen it or my trailer since I got hurt, and I want to take a look at it."

His eyebrows went up. "Perhaps you shouldn't."

I stood. "Perhaps I should. I'm going. You can either go with me or stay here."

He sighed. I swear I saw him roll his eyes. "Fine. Can I at least carry you?"

"No." I hobbled to the door. "Maybe. Only if I get too tired or I can't make it up a hill or something. I need fresh air. I need exercise. I'm ready to jump out of my skin right now and it's been a week since I had my accident. Three more weeks like this? Trust me, you won't want to be near me if I can't get out and get moving a bit."

I headed out, the war demon behind me.

"Turn left. Head up the path, then turn left after the blackberry bush." He followed me, close enough that he could catch me if I fell, but far enough away that he didn't seem like he was hovering over me.

I shuffled along, breathing heavy and sweating by the time I took that left at the blackberry bush.

And this time it really was sweat.

I barely recognized my truck when it finally came into view. It didn't even look like a truck. I looked up, up the steep, rock-strewn hill, past the smashed saplings and crushed bushes, up over what had been a breathtakingly sheer drop from the road. Then I looked at the twisted hunk of metal half buried in limbs and briars.

I cried. I cried about the loss of my beautiful truck and trailer, for the tools and forge that were somewhere scattered down this mountainside. I cried with relief that I'd somehow survived this horrific crash with minimal injuries. I could have died. I should have died. And looking at the wreck brought it all home to me.

Strong arms came around me and I leaned into Hadur's chest, not worrying about the tears and snot soaking his shirt. What miracle had allowed me to survive this crash? What miracle had made me go off the road right at Hadur's spot, sent me crashing into the woods inside the confines of his summoning circle? If the truck had come to a stop just ten feet farther, he would have been unable to reach me, to help me.

Surely there was an angel looking over me. Or maybe a demon.

"Let me carry you back to the cabin," Hadur rumbled. "I'll make something for you to eat. I'll brew some hot tea. I'll kiss you and take your mind off everything that saddens you."

The funny thing was, he could. Not just with sex or food or tea, but just by his presence. I was a bit of a loner, but I'd spent a week with this demon. I'd spent the whole day side-by-side with him just reading journals and spell books. And I was completely happy doing that. With him by my side, my injury wasn't a big deal. With him by my side, that tiny cabin was a home.

"I'm okay." I told him, sniffing as I pulled away. "I do want to check the truck for anything Diebin may have missed, though. And I want to check something else. I'll need your help."

"I live to serve." His voice was teasing, his hands smoothing back my hair.

"Good, because you're going to have to do a lot of the heavy lifting here. And I do mean heavy lifting."

I made my way over to the remains of my truck while Hadur pulled limbs and boulders out of my way, throwing them with admirable strength off to the side.

"You know, you're totally turning me on," I told him as I peered into the driver's side and shuddered at the scene. Blood. Glass. Mangled dashboard. Deflated airbag.

"I'll remember that. The witch likes feats of strength."

"Well, bring your feats over here, will you? I'd like you to open the hood. Or rip it off if you have to."

He shot me a sideways glance. "Planning on starting it and driving out of here?"

I laughed. "Now *that* would be magic. No, I want to see what happened to my brakes. Maybe I'm just being paranoid about the werewolves. Brake lines fail. Shit happens. I don't want to start a war over a mechanical failure."

He moved to the front of the truck, snapping off a thick branch and tossing it aside. "You'll be able to tell if it was tampered with or not?"

I shrugged. "A clean break on an otherwise solid brake line? I'm assuming so. Of course, with the truck smashed up like this, I might not be able to even *find* the brake line."

Another branch flew off to the side. I heard the squawk of metal. Hadur grunted, then the metal squawked again, the hood peeling free from the car like the skin from an orange.

"Can you make it over here to look?" Hadur asked. "I've got no idea what I'm seeing."

"Guess Diebin never brought you any issues of Popular Mechanics or Chilton manuals," I teased, carefully making my way to the front of the truck. I took good care of my vehicle. There hadn't been any brake noise, no vibration or pulling to one side when braking, no spongy brake pedal, no distinctive smell of burning brake fluid or puddles in my driveway. So, either this had been a sudden, catastrophic failure—which could happen—or someone had messed with my truck.

I leaned against what remained of my left front fender and looked down into the engine compartment. Setting the crutches aside, I bent over, trying to get closer.

"Shit. I can't...damn this broken leg. I can't get close enough to see." I straightened up with a huff of exasperation. "Forget it. This was a dumb idea. I can't crawl around under the car or get myself in the places I need to be to check this out. It's just going to have to wait."

"Let me do it," Hadur said. "Tell me what to look for, and I'll do it."

I pointed. "See that there? That's the master cylinder and the reservoir. They hold the brake fluid."

"Now you're turning *me* on," he commented, half-crawling over the car. "Here?"

"Yep, that's it. The lines are those tubes there. They lead to a combination valve, then to the wheels. There's a hydraulic control unit under the car for the lines running to the rear wheels. It's a closed system. The fluid circulates."

"Maybe they cut it by the wheels," he suggested. "If so, I'll have to flip the truck over and check from the bottom."

I loved how he casually suggested flipping the truck over, like that would take no effort at all.

"I don't think that's where the break is. If it happened by a wheel, then the fluid would leak out each time I used the brake. The others would work the first few times I applied the brake pedal, getting soft then not working at all as the fluid squeezed out the broken section by the one wheel. No, they either cut the line at all four wheels, or they cut it here by the master cylinder."

"Sounds quicker and easier to do it here," he said.

"Yep, that's what I'm thinking. A cut line, or bust the master cylinder with the reservoir, and it's all going to hell. I'd maybe get one soft braking in, then it would be pedal to the floor."

"I have no idea what that means exactly, but okay." He looked down at the master cylinder. "It looks smashed, but everything under here looks smashed."

"But was the hood smashed there? Because the hood should have a big ole dent right there if it happened from the wreck."

"The hood looks like someone took a sledge hammer to it," Hadur commented. "I'm no expert, but I can't say whether this happened in the wreck or not."

"How about the line then? Grab it and gently pull on it. See if it's not attached or cut. There should be two lines leading from the master cylinder."

His hands vanished into the engine compartment. "Yep. They're both cut. I can feel the edge of the hose attached to the master cylinder, then it just ends. It's jagged and sharp, not worn or frayed."

I let out a breath, not sure whether that was the answer I wanted to hear or not. "Okay, one more thing, please. I want to check the emergency brake line. It's a cable line, and it's separate from the hydraulic of the brake system. It goes from the emergency brake pedal, under the truck, to the back tires."

He stood up, wiping grease and dirt from his hands. "If you want me to look at that, I'm going to need to flip the truck. Which means I want you far enough away that you won't get hit by anything."

I hobbled backward until he told me I was a safe distance. Then the demon bent down and grabbed the truck, turning it on its side. Once he was sure the truck was stable, he stepped back and sent me a questioning glance.

Before I could tell him what to do, I heard a noise, a rustle in the briars off to my right. It normally wouldn't have sent up any alarms on my radar, but clearly the noise meant something different to Hadur. The demon raced toward me with inhuman speed, scooping me up and dashing back, depositing me on the other side of my wrecked truck. Then he vanished in a blur. Seconds later I heard a crashing noise followed by a yelp and a panicked voice pleading for mercy. By the time I'd struggled to my feet and peeked over the edge of the truck bed, I saw Hadur coming out of the woods, holding Stanley aloft by the back of his shirt.

CHAPTER 14

BRONWYN

The werewolf was limp in an utterly submissive pose that any other time would have been hysterical. Instead, my pulse raced to see him. My truck had been tampered with. The werewolves wanted me dead. And I wasn't sure if Cassie's threats would keep them back or not.

Why was Stanley here? Spying on us in preparation for an attack? Was he sent to take me out himself? Or spin me some lie designed to get me out of the safety of Hadur's circle and to somewhere he could kill me?

Hadur marched up to me and threw the werewolf down at my feet. "Talk," he commanded.

I flinched, for a second thinking that order was meant for me.

"Don't kill me, don't kill me," Stanley pleaded, his hands protectively over his head. "I was being noisy on purpose, so you could hear me coming. I need to talk to you. I need to tell you something. So don't kill me."

Good grief. When had Stanley become such a wimp? "I can't vouch for Hadur, but I don't have any immediate plans to kill you, so talk."

The werewolf glanced around. "Can we go somewhere more private? The cabin?"

I nodded. Hadur went to grab Stanley, no doubt to perp-walk him back to the cabin, then he hesitated, looking at my leg.

"I can walk," I told him. Then I realized something. "Well, I could if you hadn't rushed me over here without my crutches."

It wasn't just the crutches, either. I was on the opposite side of the truck with no clear and easy way to get back to the path. The demon did a back and forth between the were-wolf and me.

"Carry me over to my crutches," I told Hadur. "Stanley, you make one wrong move and I'll curse you bald for the next six months."

I couldn't do curses, but Stanley didn't know that. He blanched, reaching up to touch his thick beard. Werewolves were hairy—like really hairy. Even the women. It didn't make them much fun at the pool in the summer, but having a chest and back that looked like a throw rug was a source of pride to them. The more hair, the better—legs, back, face, chest. The works. Being hairless would send Stanley into a humiliated self-imposed isolation for six months. It was an effective threat, even if it was a threat I had no ability to carry out.

Hadur picked me up, taking me to my crutches then hovering protectively by me as I got things organized and made my way down the path. He followed with Stanley's arm held firmly in his grasp. Back at the cabin, I sank into a chair, worn out from my exertions. Hadur made Stanley stand over by the door, then went to pour me some tea.

The werewolf fidgeted. "I could be killed for this, you know. If it gets out that I warned you, that I was involved in any of this, I won't be safe either in Dallas' pack or Clinton's.

If I need help, can I rely on the witches to give me sanctuary? Like they did with Shelby?"

Pack law didn't allow for lone wolves. It also didn't allow the females to have sexual relations with anyone but a male werewolf. Shelby had gotten herself in a pickle by falling in love with a female troll. Clinton had been about to rat her out to Dallas, so rather than face a forced mating and a lifetime confined to the pack compound, Shelby had decided to eliminate Clinton and keep her secret a secret.

Luckily, Clinton had survived. Luckily Cassie had felt sorry for Shelby and decided to bend the human law our town based its governance on and call the whole thing aggravated assault. Shelby got community service, but she also got a sort of refugee status in the town. She was a lone wolf, unaffiliated with either pack. There would be no reprisal for either Shelby's attack on Clinton or her relationship with Alberta. Any wolf who decided to take the law into his own hands would face Cassie. And no one wanted to face Cassie when she was pissed off.

Did I mention she'd once set her ex-boyfriend's pants on fire? In the middle of the courthouse? Yeah. Don't piss off my sister.

That's what Stanley was bargaining for. Being a lone wolf wasn't all sunshine and roses, though. I knew Shelby. I hung out with her and Alberta sometimes. The werewolf was depressed, missing her pack. As far as they were concerned, she wasn't even a werewolf. They completely ignored her. No werewolf was allowed to speak to her or acknowledge her presence. She'd been shunned, and that had been a hard price to pay for love.

It made me realize how much Stanley was risking to talk to us. Death, or shunning. Either one horrible.

"We'll protect you, Stanley," I told him, hoping it didn't come to that. Although maybe if he got shunned, Shelby would finally have a werewolf to hang with. I mean, she'd hated Stanley before, but surely he'd be better than nothing at all?

He nodded and clasped his hands in front of him. "It's not Dallas, it's Clinton. Although Clinton will deny it and say it's some rogue in his group operating without his knowledge or consent. Some poor wolf will lose his life if it comes to that, and Clinton will insist justice was done."

"What the hell is he talking about?" Hadur asked as he handed me a cup of tea.

"I think he's saying Clinton had my truck tampered with in an attempt to kill me, right?" I took a sip of my tea and regarded the werewolf. The fact that Stanley knew this meant he was some sort of werewolf double agent—living with Dallas' pack, but obviously in the know and facilitating things with Clinton's. The werewolf had more guts than I'd thought.

Stanley nodded. "Clinton didn't expect you to die. He just wanted you to wreck. You'd find out your brakes had been cut and figure one of Dallas' wolves had done it. Then your sister would go up there and rip Dallas' spine out his ass."

I winced at the visual. "So, Clinton was setting it up to look like Dallas tried to have me killed?"

"Yeah, but it didn't work. It took you too long to fix the butchering equipment up at the compound. With the storm and the rockslide, you went over the hill. We figured you were dead, that when your sister eventually found you, she'd just assume it was an accident."

"And none of the blame would have gone to Dallas," Hadur finished.

"So, wait," I interrupted. "Clinton was happy to just let my body lay there in a wrecked truck for days until Cassie found it? Seriously?"

Stanley looked down at the floor. "If he'd reported the

wreck, it would have looked suspicious. This part of the mountain isn't where he and the splinter group of wolves have laid claim to. He'd have no reason to be over here. And the way your truck went down, you can't see it from the road. So Clinton couldn't report it without looking suspicious, and Dallas didn't even know. Dallas just figured a rockslide took out some of the road and had us clear it. He never checked down the hill."

I scowled, very unhappy that Stanley hadn't found some way of alerting the pack that I was down here. Or sending an anonymous tip to one of my sisters or something.

"Then why did you come last time?" Hadur growled, taking a menacing step toward the werewolf. "You told us Dallas sent you to get Bronwyn."

Stanley cringed. "He did send me. He got your message and sent me down to bring Bronwyn to the compound. That way he could deliver her to Cassandra, make like he'd rescued her and cared for her. And then Cassandra would be grateful and get off his back. Instead you refused to turn her over, then Cassandra came up to the compound and read Dallas the riot act, threatening to kill him if her sister has so much as a broken finger nail. I'm lucky he didn't kill me over that."

I suddenly realized where all this was going. "Dallas has a spy in his compound—a spy besides you, that is. And that spy went to Clinton and told him about Cassie's threats."

Stanley nodded. "And Clinton's got a second chance to make his plan work. All he needs to do is attack you, make it look like Dallas did it, then he'll be pack alpha over all of Heartbreak Mountain while Dallas is rotting in a grave somewhere."

"This Clinton plans to kill Bronwyn?" Hadur's voice was low and quiet. Stanley shivered and arched his back, hunching low.

"It doesn't matter whether she lives or dies," Stanley told him. "If she's attacked and hurt, then she'll tell her sister it was the werewolves and Cassandra will go straight to Dallas. If she's killed, then Cassandra will find out and know who to blame."

I sucked in a breath. "When is this attack supposed to occur, Stanley?"

The werewolf glanced up at me, clearly miserable. "Tonight. Probably around midnight because that's always the best time for an attack."

Werewolves. So predictable. "What's going to happen?" I asked.

"About a dozen wolves are supposed to hit hard and fast and draw the big guy away. Then another three are supposed to come in the other side, into the cabin to rough you up. Everyone is supposed to be in and out in less than twenty minutes. Hit hard and fast, then get the hell out before anyone gets killed. And if a wolf goes down, they have orders to haul him out, even if it's a body."

"Leave no proof behind that it's Clinton's wolves and not Dallas'," I commented.

"I need to get back." Stanley edged backward toward the door. "They'll already scent that I was here. Clinton's gonna know I warned you. Dallas is gonna wonder what I'm doing down here. I'm screwed. I'm so screwed."

"I think you need to spend the night in town," I told him. "Grab some buddies, head to Pistol Pete's or the Tavern, then get a room at Hollister's Inn or sleep on someone's couch."

He shot Hadur a quick glance to make sure the demon was in agreement with that, then quickly made his exit. I finished my tea, then tried to think.

This sucked. I couldn't leave. Even if I managed to get a message to Ophelia and she somehow arranged to have me airlifted out of here before nightfall, I couldn't leave Hadur here to handle this by himself. What should I do? I glanced over at the demon, wondering if I could get a message to Cassie, get all my sisters to come here and make a stand with us. The seven of us witches, plus two demons? We'd be a force no werewolf would want to face.

Hadur shook his head, as if reading my mind. "They'd know, and they'd just delay. We can't have your sisters here every night for four weeks until you heal and leave. Perhaps you should consider having your sister fly you back to the town, where you'll be safe."

I ached to hear him say that. "I'm safe with you," I told him. "I'm a witch. And I've got the nipper-wand and a bunch of enchanted spoons in addition to the magic Cassie laid down before she left. If the attack happens as Stanley said, then you take care of the werewolves in the woods, and I'll handle whoever makes it to the cabin. If I can't fight off three werewolves, then I probably deserve to get my ass beat."

"I don't want you fighting off three werewolves, not injured like you are. If one of them gets close enough to grab you, your leg won't be the only thing broken. No, if you're insisting we make a stand, we're going to make it together."

"Then we'll have fifteen werewolves attacking us," I told him. "I'm worried they'll try to burn down the cabin or something."

"They won't," Hadur smiled down at me. "That would bring not only Dallas' wolves running, but whoever manages your fire department in the town as well. Their goal is to frame Dallas. And the motive they're putting on Dallas for this is revenge and trying to get you witches to back off and let him do his thing without oversight."

"Well, Clinton's an idiot, because Cassie would see right through that. She'd be pissed at first and blame Dallas, but then she'd come to her senses and realize that Dallas isn't going to hurt me, not after the threat she delivered. It's like poking the bear, and he might be an arrogant ass, but Dallas isn't dumb enough to poke the bear."

"And he's most likely not dumb enough to set his own mountain on fire to hurt a witch he doesn't really care about and piss off a witch that could probably kill him." Hadur shook his head. "I agree. This Clinton isn't very smart."

"Poor werewolves. Two crappy choices in their alphas. Maybe if they didn't pick their leaders through violent combat and instead voted, or had them play Old Maid, or do rock-paper-scissors, they might actually have a chance of a decent leader."

"Sounds like they need a revolution," Hadur commented.

I glared at him. "No wars. They've already got one. Do not go inciting any additional wars among the werewolf packs."

He snorted. "Doesn't sound like they need my help on that front. Besides, not all revolutions are violent, and war does not always end with the physically strongest as the winner."

I folded my arms across my chest. "No war."

"Not even a little tiny one?"

"No."

He grinned. "Fine. I'll just have to satisfy myself with killing fifteen werewolves tonight."

"And no killing the werewolves."

That wiped the smile from his face. "What do you mean? They'll be attacking me. Their purpose is to harm, or possibly kill, you. Even that spoiled demon bonded to your sister would agree that killing them is justice served."

"Well, I *don't* agree. I like some of these werewolves. They've got Dallas Dickskin on one hand and Clinton Dickskin on the other. It's time to show some mercy. Beat them up. Send them running. Don't kill them."

Hadur stared at me. "Their name is Dickskin? Seriously? Dickskin?"

"Yep. Dickskin."

"Well, then, I agree. We should definitely show mercy on anyone who had to pledge loyalty to a werewolf with the last name of Dickskin."

"Good. We're on the same page. Now let's relax, conserve our energy, and get ready to fight."

He bowed, the grin returning to his face. "I live to serve, my witch."

CHAPTER 15

BRONWYN

*A*s Stanley had said, the attack came at midnight. Hadur had sent Diebin into town on an errand, telling him not to come back until morning. We'd watched the fat raccoon run off through the woods, and I'd entwined my fingers with the demon's, delighted that he'd been so concerned about his raccoon familiar's safety.

I was glad Diebin was safely away, because the prospect of eighteen werewolves attacking us here in our home was nearly giving me a panic attack.

I stood as the alarm sounded, refusing to fight from a bed or a chair. But in my case, standing meant having crutches under my arms for balance just in case I needed to quickly hop across the room. I positioned myself near the table, where I'd lined up my enchanted spoons and the nipper-wand.

Hadur paced, anger practically rolling off him in waves. When the wolves crossed the perimeter of the summoning circle, he knew it. I knew it too, thanks to the alarms Cassie had placed along the magical barrier.

I tried to calm my breathing while Hadur moved to stand

in front of me. It was sweet, really it was, but he was completely blocking my view of the one entrance to the cabin and thus my ability to throw any magic at intruding werewolves.

"Uh, babe? I can't throw a spoon through your body, so you need to move over."

He edged over a few feet.

"More. My accuracy in throwing shit isn't major league. It would really suck if I hit you with a spoon or a charge from the nipper-wand."

That got me another six feet of space. It would have to do, because they were coming, stomping like elephants through the forest, howling and shouting, no doubt trying to draw Hadur out of the cabin so the other three could circle around and smack the crap out of me.

Hadur's hands curled into fists. I could tell it was all he could do to keep from charging out the door and taking these guys down. The air in the cabin crackled with his magic, and his eyes glowed an eerie amber. What was he doing? Was this just his energy spilling out because of the pending conflict, or was he actually using his demon skills?

Bright lights flashed outside the small window. I heard yelps and grinned, knowing that Cassie's spelled flashlight had done its job. It also meant that the wolves were close. They were done waiting for Hadur to come to them, and instead had decided to come to us.

Idiots.

I exchanged a quick glance with the war demon and picked up a spoon in each hand. The door flew open. Three werewolves charged in, immediately jumping on Hadur. More werewolves streamed through the door, joining the other three and quickly overwhelming the demon.

I threw two spoons, shouting "sit" with each one. Two werewolves fell to the floor, instantly as weak as pups.

"Get the witch," one of the wolves yelled.

Shit. I pivoted, shifting my focus from defending Hadur to defending myself. Four more wolves went down before I ran out of spoons and had to resort to the nipper-wand.

Three of the wolves that were on Hadur flew across the room, smashing into the log walls with a heavy thud. More wolves were trying to push their way into the cabin. Between the ones fighting and the ones on the floor, we were running out of space. I edged backward, brandishing the nipper-wand, thinking that instead of being beaten, I was most likely going to be crushed.

Two wolves rushed me. I dropped one with a shot from the nipper-wand and barely managed to down the other before he reached me. The wolves I'd hit with the spoons were beginning to get up and return to the fray. I backed away until my ass hit the wall, trying desperately to keep the attacking werewolves at a wand's distance. Too late I realized that the wolves had deliberately separated us—Hadur at one end of the small cabin and me at the other, eighteen wolves in between us.

Three werewolves rushed me, one grabbing my arm. I hit him with the nipper-wand, the charge cycling through the wolf and into me. He yelped, I shrieked. The demon energy in the room surged, and suddenly I wasn't sure what was the electrical zap of the wand and what was whatever Hadur was doing.

"Brad, you worthless cheating dog," one of the were-wolves snarled, grabbing the one that was trying to wrestle me to the ground in spite of the electrical charge I'd just zapped him with.

Brad turned around, his eyes narrowed. "Tenny, get your damned hairy paws off me right now. If you were less of a frigid bitch, I wouldn't have to sleep around."

Tenny snarled and dove at Brad, her hands curling into

claws, her mouth lengthening into a snout full of sharp teeth. I squeaked and got out of their way as they tore into each other just like two mastiffs fighting over a bone. It was then that I realized Tenny and Brad weren't the only ones. Instead of attacking me and Hadur, the werewolves had turned on each other.

And they were making a mess of our cabin.

I looked across the room at Hadur. "Get them out of here before they wreck the place!" I shouted.

He held up his hands. "I can only make them fight, not leave."

Great. Guess that made me the bouncer then.

"Get out, get out," I yelled, zapping werewolves with my nipper-wand. Hadur followed my lead, whacking werewolves out the door with one of the chairs. I hobbled on one crutch, continuing to shoot werewolves until my nipper-wand was out of charge.

Once all the wolves were outside, Hadur closed the door and turned to me.

"We did it," I told him.

"We did it until the next time." He scowled. "It's not safe here for you. Come morning, I want that sister of yours to fly you out of here and back to the town where you'll be safe. I can take care of these curs on my own."

"Hey, it's not like I stood in the corner and screamed. I helped. In fact, I more than helped. I kicked some serious werewolf ass, and I could do it again."

"You can't keep fighting off werewolves with a broken leg." He was in front of me in three strides, pulling me into his arms. "I was terrified that they'd harm you before I managed to get them to turn on each other. I was so afraid they'd injure or even kill you. I can handle any attack they bring to my door, but not if I'm worried about your safety."

I reached up to touch his face. "We run this town, Hadur.

We witches are the authority for everything that happens inside our wards. Cassie has just started taking her place as head witch. The werewolves will fall in line or face exile, and it's not going to be long before they realize that none of us witches are going to back down. *I'm* not going to back down."

"If anything were to happen to you…"

"Cassie will go deliver an epic smack-down to Clinton and his pack, and what happened tonight will never happen again. Clinton is a pansy. He doesn't want to take Cassie on. His whole plan here was to pit my sister against Dallas to gain control of the mountain. We'll send Diebin in with a note come morning. Cassie will do her thing, and I'll stay here for however long it takes me to get you out of this summoning circle."

He kissed the top of my head and held me close. "I do want to tell you how magnificent you were tonight. You with your back against the wall, bright pink cast on your leg, throwing spoons and zapping werewolves with a spelled farrier tool…it was damned sexy."

"Even the pink cast?" I asked, my words muffled against his shirt.

"Especially the pink cast," he murmured. Then he bent his head and kissed me.

It was a gentle kiss, then something sparked and he groaned, pulling me against him and parting my lips with his tongue tasting, licking, and…ravaging. Yes, that was the word. Ravaging. His tongue teased mine, then he pulled away to catch a breath. I yanked him back to me, nibbling on his bottom lip and tugging it with my teeth as I dug my fingers into his hair. His hands slid down my back to cup my ass, pulling me up against his erection as he took over, kissing me once more. My world fell away, and all I knew was his mouth on mine.

"Hey! Is everyone okay in here?" Cassie's cheerful voice rang out from the doorway. I pulled away from Hadur and glared at her. My sister, worst timing in the whole world.

"Wow, I'm really not a fan of the redecorating effort here." She grinned over at me. "I'm guessing you're okay. Either that, or your demon was busy checking your tonsils for damage there."

"We're fine. Pull up a chair and let me tell you about the eighteen werewolves we just fought off, though."

"I know." Cassie righted one of the chairs and sat down. "Ophelia called me in a panic because she'd had a vision. Then I panicked and Lucien and I drove up here at speeds Jeff Gordon would have envied. Lucien grabbed four of the werewolves crawling their way through the woods. Nice job with the wand, by the way. I totally want you to make me one of those, only not on a tool. Maybe something like a judge's gavel or a silver candlestick."

"I'll get right on that," I drawled.

"Good. Anyway, Lucien and I had a chat with the werewolves we grabbed, and let's just say I plan on paying a visit to Clinton Dickskin first thing in the morning."

I shot Hadur a knowing glance. "So we're good here?"

"You're good." Cassie waved a hand. "Go back to swapping bodily fluids. Lucien and I are going to head home with a quick pitstop at the Accident jail. He's got those four werewolves, or maybe more by now, and I'm thinking there are some assault as well as breaking and entering charges about to be filed. The werewolves are going to learn that this kind of thing is going to result in a whole lot of legal trouble."

Leave it to my sister, the lawyer and the head witch of Accident, to step up to the plate and handle this like a pro.

Leave it to Cassie to once again take care of her family, to make us all feel safe, to let me know she had it all in hand.

My sister headed out into the night and I turned once more to Hadur.

"So, can I stay? Are you satisfied that there won't be any further threat on my life?"

He smiled down at me. "Yes. And I'm happy to have you stay with me for as long as you want."

I smiled back. "Good. Now...where were we before my sister so rudely interrupted us?"

CHAPTER 16

"*R*eady?" I looked over at my demon.

"Ready." Hadur took a breath and went to stand at the edge of the summoning circle while I crossed over the line to the other side.

Six weeks I'd lived here with him in this cabin. Six weeks of what felt like a honeymoon to me. Well, not quite a honeymoon with my sisters in and out every few days, but probably the closest I'd ever get to one. My leg had healed, and with Ophelia and Glenda's help, I was almost back to normal as far as mobility was concerned. My sisters joked that I'd never truly be normal, but then again, they weren't exactly normal themselves.

Hadur and I had pored over spell books in the cabin, and my sisters had done the same in their homes. Hundreds of years of Perkins witches made for a whole lot of books, and the spidery writing wasn't always that easy to read. We never did find Celesta's missing spell book, but we did find that Temperance herself had noted several rituals for summoning and banishing demons in an ancient spell book—each entry with quite a few admonishments that future generations should avoid these at all costs. Evidently Temperance was not fond of hellspawn.

I, on the other hand, was fond of one particular hellspawn. And let me tell you, we'd done a whole lot more in six weeks than read spell books. Holy moly, that demon could seriously rock my world in bed. Rock. My. World.

"You sure this is gonna work?" Cassie asked as I took my place beside her. Each of my sisters was stationed at a key point around the summoning circle, each ready to contribute her energy.

"It's this or banishment, and that's not an option," I replied.

"It might eventually be the only option," she told me with a sad smile.

I knew what she meant. If this didn't work, then we'd still continue our quest to find a spell to free Hadur, and in the meantime I'd live with him here. If we never found the spell, a future generation of witches would need to banish Hadur after my death.

Or not. If I bonded with him as Cassie and Lucien were planning to do, I would live forever as some sort of demon witch, either here or in hell. It was an idea I was beginning to embrace. Hadur and I, together. Forever. The thought made me ridiculously happy.

With a nod to Cassie, I lit my candle. She did the same, calling out the words to create a magical space. I heard each sister do the same in turn, felt the magic snap around us like a band, a circle on top of another circle.

"Let what is old fall away, and the new remain," I said. "Let the power of our circle draw its strength from the old. Let both become one."

We began to chant, the energy humming and pulsing. I felt the circles join together, felt the bonds that held Hadur in place merge with what we had created.

Then I began the ritual—the summoning ritual from Temperance's spell book. With my sisters holding the circle in their chant, I traced Hadur's sigil upon the ground and called him forth from hell.

Only he wasn't in hell. He was already here, just twenty feet away. A new summoning to take the place of the old. I only hoped it would work.

Hadur stepped forward. "Who summons me and for what purpose?"

"I, Bronwyn Perkins, witch of Accident, summon you. In accordance with this ancient rite, I command you to do my bidding. Complete the task I request of you, and you shall be free to remain here or return to hell."

That was another long shot. The ritual had the demon immediately returning to hell upon completion of the task. I hoped that my re-wording things didn't screw anything up.

"I will obey, my witch. Tell me my task, so that I may perform it and be free."

I pointed to the ground beside me. "Your task is to bring me that rock."

Cassie snickered, then slapped a hand over her mouth. With an apologetic glance, she continued chanting.

"That rock?" Hadur gave me a strange look.

"Yes. That rock. I want that rock. Your task is to retrieve it and give it to me."

"I accept the task, my witch." He took a step forward and hesitated, eyeing me uncertainly.

Here it was. He'd told me when he touched the invisible barrier of the summoning circle, it was painful. It shocked him, hurt him like nothing in hell ever had, like a thousand barbed needles stabbing and ripping at his flesh. This was the moment of truth. He'd either pass through the circle, or be in agony on the other side.

The demon took a breath and walked forward. I felt the

energy of the circle shimmer, tense, coil as if it were a snake about to strike. Then it allowed him through.

He walked to my side, bent down to pick up the rock, and handed it to me. "My task is done, Bronwyn Perkins, witch of Accident."

"Yes, your task is done, Hadur, my demon." I launched myself into his arms, slipping the rock into my pocket. Then I kissed him and left my sisters to dismiss the magical circle, leaving nothing but woods, a wrecked truck, and a cabin here. The lack of magic seemed odd, empty and hollow.

No, I was wrong. It was far from empty. There would always be something magical about this place. It would always feel like home to me.

"I can't wait for you to see my home—our home," I told Hadur.

"I can't wait to see everything," he replied. "Your home, your work, your friends. I can't wait to have Sunday dinner with your noisy and somewhat obnoxious family and that spoiled pompous demon who has attached himself to your sister. I can't wait to spend each day and night with you, my beloved witch."

Me too. Oh, me too. There was a rustle in a nearby briar and out popped a giant, fat raccoon. I bent down and picked Diebin up, knowing that we wouldn't be a family without the little guy. "Ready to go home?" I asked him.

He chattered, then squirmed free from my arms, heading up toward the road where our cars were parked. Me. A demon. A raccoon. Funny how life had taken a turn for the better when I'd crashed down this mountain.

"Hey," I asked Hadur as we walked up the hill hand-in-hand. "Do you think Diebin would be okay if we got a cat?"

ACKNOWLEDGMENTS

Thanks to my copyeditors Erin Zarro and Jennifer Cosham whose eagle eyes catch all the typos and keep my comma problem in line, and to Renee George for cover design.

ABOUT THE AUTHOR

Debra lives in a little house in the woods of Maryland with her sons and two slobbery bloodhounds. On a good day, she jogs and horseback rides, hopefully managing to keep the horse between herself and the ground. Her only known super power is 'Identify Roadkill'.

For more information:
www.debradunbar.com
Debra Dunbar's Author page

ALSO BY DEBRA DUNBAR

Accidental Witches Series
Brimstone and Broomsticks
Warmongers and Wands (Feb 2019)
Death and Divination (March 2019)

White Lightning Series
Wooden Nickels
Bum's Rush
Clip Joint
Jake Walk
Trouble Boys (2019)

***

The Templar Series
Dead Rising
Last Breath
Bare Bones
Famine's Feast
Royal Blood (2019)
Dark Crossroads (2019)

* * *

IMP WORLD NOVELS

The Imp Series

A Demon Bound

Satan's Sword

Elven Blood

Devil's Paw

Imp Forsaken

Angel of Chaos

Kingdom of Lies

Exodus

Queen of the Damned

The Morning Star

* * *

Half-breed Series

Demons of Desire

Sins of the Flesh

Cornucopia

Unholy Pleasures

City of Lust

* * *

Imp World Novels

No Man's Land

Stolen Souls

Three Wishes

Northern Lights

Far From Center

Penance

* * *

Printed in the USA
CPSIA information can be obtained
at www.ICGtesting.com
LVHW091359150824
788346LV00006B/84

9 781952 216312